MAN
ARMOR WARS

FOUNTAINDALE PUB
300 West
Bolingbrook, IL
(630)

WRITER: **JOE CARAMAGNA**
ARTIST: **CRAIG ROUSSEAU**
COLORIST: **VAL STAPLES**
LETTERER: **DAVE SHARPE**
COVER ARTISTS: **SKOTTIE YOUNG, FRANCIS TSAI & TAKESHI MIYAZAWA**
ASSISTANT EDITOR: **MICHAEL HORWITZ**
EDITOR: **NATHAN COSBY**

COLLECTION EDITOR: **CORY LEVINE**
ASSISTANT EDITORS: **ALEX STARBUCK & JOHN DENNING**
EDITORS, SPECIAL PROJECTS: **JENNIFER GRÜNWALD & MARK D. BEAZLEY**
SENIOR EDITOR, SPECIAL PROJECTS: **JEFF YOUNGQUIST**
SENIOR VICE PRESIDENT OF SALES: **DAVID GABRIEL**

EDITOR IN CHIEF: **JOE QUESADA**
PUBLISHER: **DAN BUCKLEY**
EXECUTIVE PRODUCER: **ALAN FINE**

1

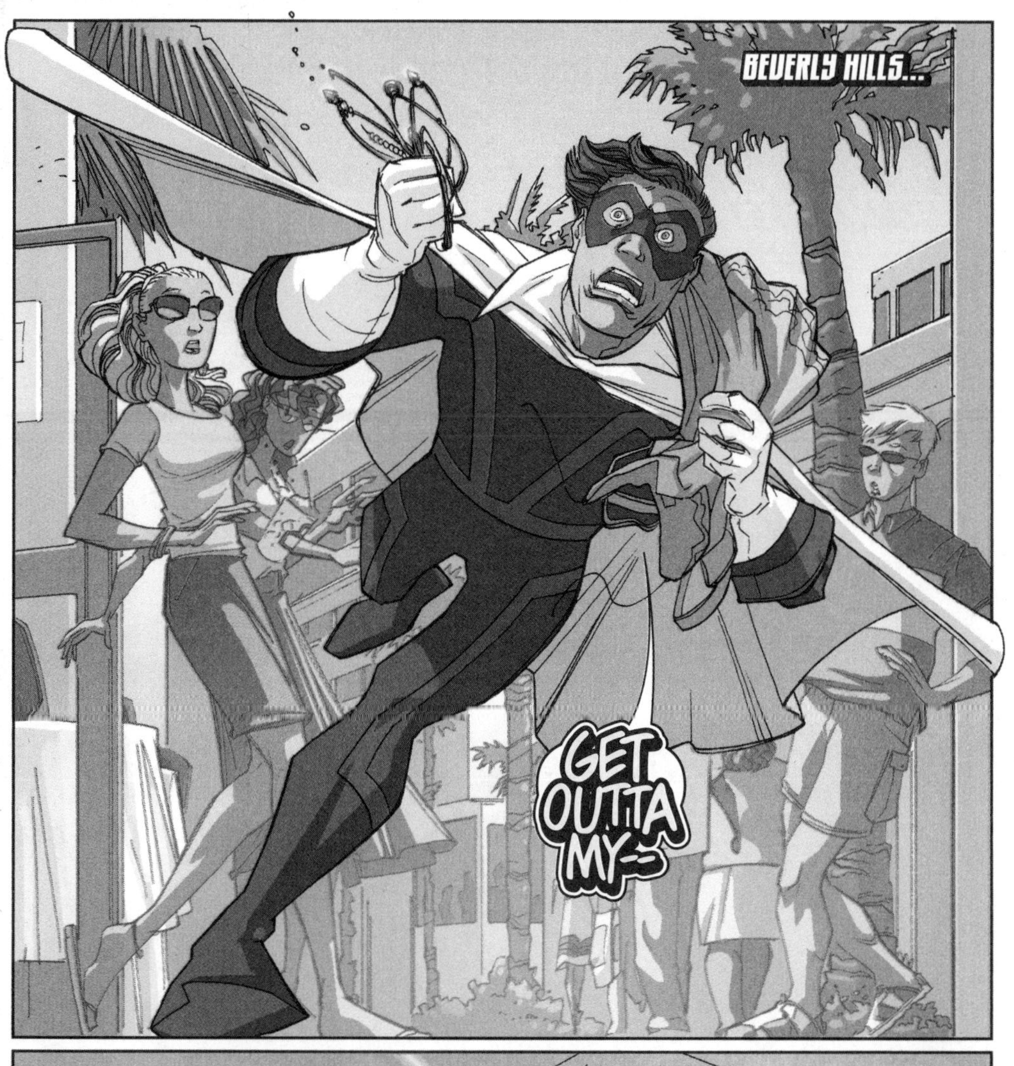
BEVERLY HILLS...
GET OUTTA MY--

WAY

VROOOOOOOOOOOOSH!
RETINAL SCAN I.D. CONFIRMED...
...NAME: CARLTON SANDERS. ALIAS: TRUMP...
...KNOWN CRIMINAL RECORD IN THE UNITED STATES...
...OCCUPATION: STAGE MAGICIAN...
...POWERS: NONE.
GULP!
HUH.
POOF
HEY! THERE HE GOES!
REPULSOR BEAM: ARMED.

REPULSOR INTENSITY: 2.6%
HRRR...!
HAND IT OVER.
I DON'T HAVE IT...
...IT'S BEHIND YOUR EAR.
TAAA-DAAAAAA...
--AHEM-- THE OTHER ONE, TOO.
PTOO!
GOOD BOY.
STRENGTH LEVEL: 1.2%. CONTACT INITIATED.
BDONK
IRON MAN!

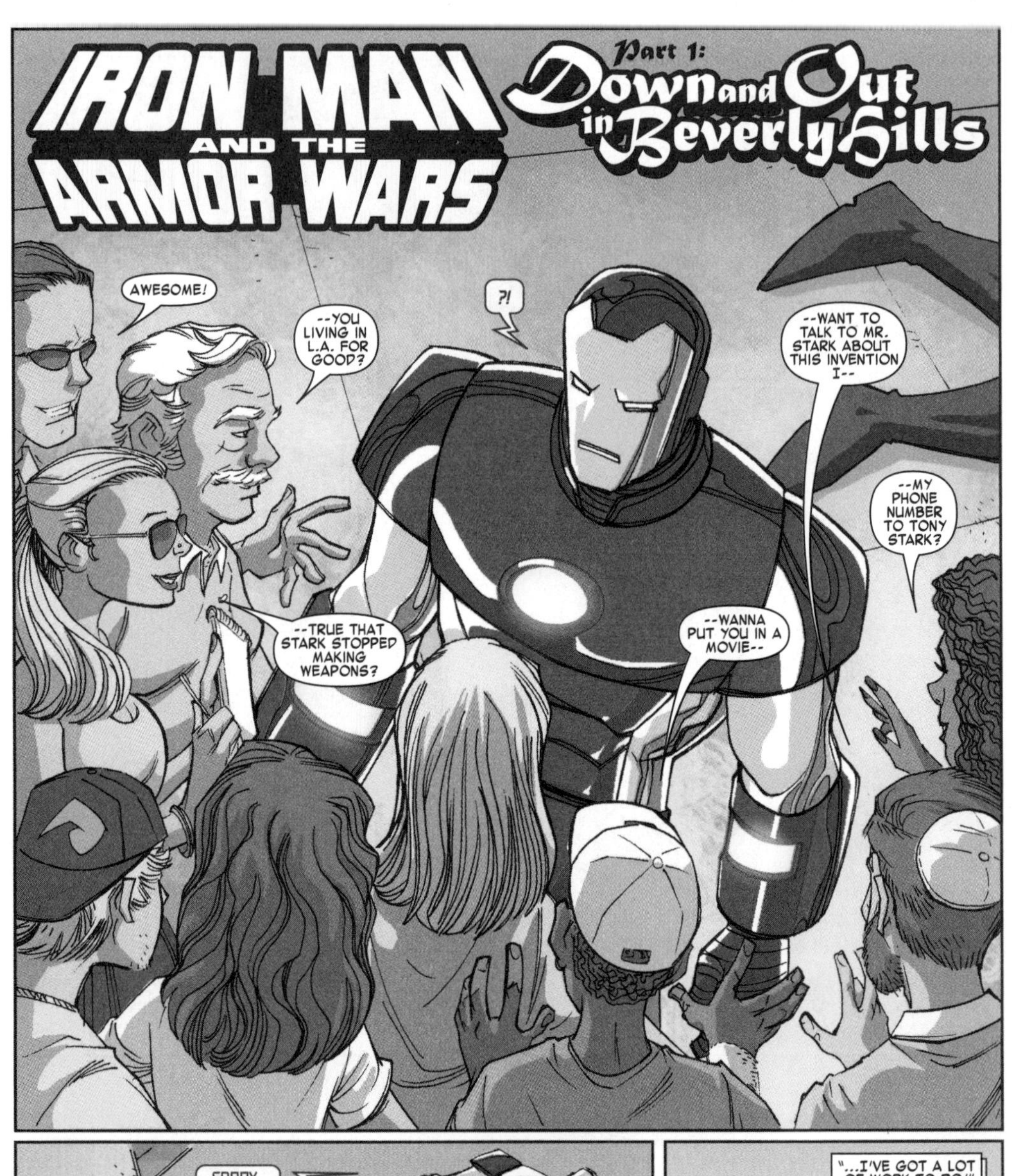
IRON MAN AND THE ARMOR WARS
Part 1: Down and Out in Beverly Hills
AWESOME!
--YOU LIVING IN L.A. FOR GOOD?
?!
--WANT TO TALK TO MR. STARK ABOUT THIS INVENTION I--
--MY PHONE NUMBER TO TONY STARK?
--TRUE THAT STARK STOPPED MAKING WEAPONS?
--WANNA PUT YOU IN A MOVIE--

SORRY, EVERYONE, I GOTTA RUN...
BOOT JETS ACTIVATED. FORCE: 10.2%.
NOOOOO!
COME BACK!

"...I'VE GOT A LOT OF WORK TO DO!"
KNOCK
KNOCK
KNOCK
KNOCK

FORGET YOUR SWIPE CARD AGAIN?
I'M TONY STARK, A.K.A. IRON MAN. BUT THAT'S MY SECRET.
SOME WOULD SAY I'M A BRILLIANT INVENTOR-- A REAL AMERICAN HERO.
OTHERS'D SAY I'M A SPOILED PLAYBOY WHO ONLY CARES ABOUT HAVING A GOOD TIME.
THEY'D ALL BE RIGHT.
I COME BEARING GIFTS.
JIM "RHODEY" RHODES IS MY BUSINESS ASSOCIATE, CONFIDANT, AND BEST FRIEND.
WE GO WAY BACK. HE KNOWS MY SECRET.
PIZZA!
PIZZA!
CONGRATULATIONS, TONE. THERE'S NEWS ABOUT YOU NOT IN THE GOSSIP SECTION.
HAR HAR. SHUT UP AND TELL ME WHAT IT SAYS.
"BILLIONAIRE INDUSTRIALIST TONY STARK--"
--SNICKER--
"--WILL REVEAL THE FIRST MAJOR PRODUCT OF THE NEW LOS ANGELES-BASED STARK ENTERPRISES TONIGHT IN THE ATRIUM OF THE LAYTON HOTEL"...BLAH, BLAH, BLAH...
..."THE AS-YET-UNNAMED PRODUCT HAS BEEN A TOPIC OF POLITICAL DEBATE, WITH MANY WONDERING WHY FEDERAL DOLLARS ARE BEING WASTED ON A WEAPONS MANUFACTURER THAT NO LONGER MANUFACTURES WEAPONS..."
MMM.

"--ESPECIALLY SINCE MOST FINANCIAL EXPERTS HAVE ALREADY PREDICTED ITS DEMISE."
EH, WHAT DO THEY KNOW? LOS ANGELES IS A LONG WAY FROM WALL STREET.
IT SURE IS.
...
YOU THINK MOVING HERE WAS A MISTAKE?
WELL, LET'S SEE.
WE'VE BEEN HERE SIX MONTHS. WE'VE GOT ONE CONTRACT THAT'S COSTING US MORE THAN WE'VE MADE SO FAR, OTHER PRODUCTS THAT ARE GOING NOWHERE, AND A STAFF WE CAN'T AFFORD TO PAY.
SO...IS THAT A YES OR A NO?
THE PENTAGON KEEPS ASKING ABOUT WEAPONS...
ABSOLUTELY NOT.
BUT, TONY...
...IT'S ONLY NATURAL-- YOU'RE THE BEST WEAPONS MAKER ON THE PLANET--
YOU MEAN, I WAS...

...UNTIL THE PEOPLE WHO BOUGHT THEM FROM ME TURNED AROUND AND SOLD THEM TO THOSE WITH BAD INTENTIONS. I MADE WEAPONS TO DEFEND OUR FREEDOM, NOT KILL INNOCENT PEOPLE...
...AND I'LL DIE BEFORE I EVER LET ANY OF MY INVENTIONS BE USED FOR EVIL AGAIN!

FINE. I WON'T BRING IT UP ANY-MORE. BUT THE PAYROLL--
TRANSFER FUNDS FROM ANOTHER INVESTMENT TO COVER NEXT WEEK'S EXPENSES. IT DOESN'T MATTER, BECAUSE AFTER TONIGHT...

...WE'LL NEVER HAVE TO WORRY ABOUT THAT EVER AGAIN.
SPEAKING OF TONIGHT--

--YOU'D BETTER GO GET CLEANED UP, YOU LOOK LIKE TEN MILES OF BAD ROAD. I'LL GET THIS ALL OVER TO THE LAYTON AND MAKE SURE SECURITY'S AIRTIGHT.
DON'T YOU WORRY ABOUT A THING.
THANKS, RHODEY.
YOU NEVER REALLY GAVE ME AN ANSWER...

...DO YOU THINK IT WAS A MISTAKE TO MOVE OUT HERE?
GOOD QUESTION, TONE...
"...I GUESS WE'LL FIND OUT TONIGHT."
YOWW!
DO THAT AGAIN...
...AND YOU'LL BE PICKING PIECES OF MY HEEL OUT OF YOUR TEETH!
SORRY, MISS POTTS!
LADIES AND GENTLEMEN...

...PUT YOUR HANDS TOGETHER FOR THE ONE, THE ONLY...
TONNNYYYYYYYY STARK!
OH, GIVE ME A BREAK...

TON-Y!
TON-Y!
TON-Y!
TON-Y!
THANK YOU L.A.! YOU'RE WAY TOO KIND.

NO, SERIOUSLY-- NO, PLEASE...IT'S EMBARRASSING!
I BET!
WHEN I MOVED OUT HERE, A LOT OF PEOPLE SAID MY NEW BUSINESS COULDN'T MAKE IT IN HOLLYWOOD-- THERE ARE TOO MANY TEMPTATIONS OUT HERE FOR A GUY LIKE ME.

INSTEAD, I'VE BEEN MORE MOTIVATED AND FOCUSED THESE PAST SIX MONTHS THAN EVER BEFORE.
AND TONIGHT, YOU'LL SEE THE FRUITS OF THIS LABOR--
--THE GREATEST THING TO EVER HAPPEN TO THE MILITARY AND LAW ENFORCEMENT AGENCIES OF THE U.S. AND ITS ALLIES ABROAD...

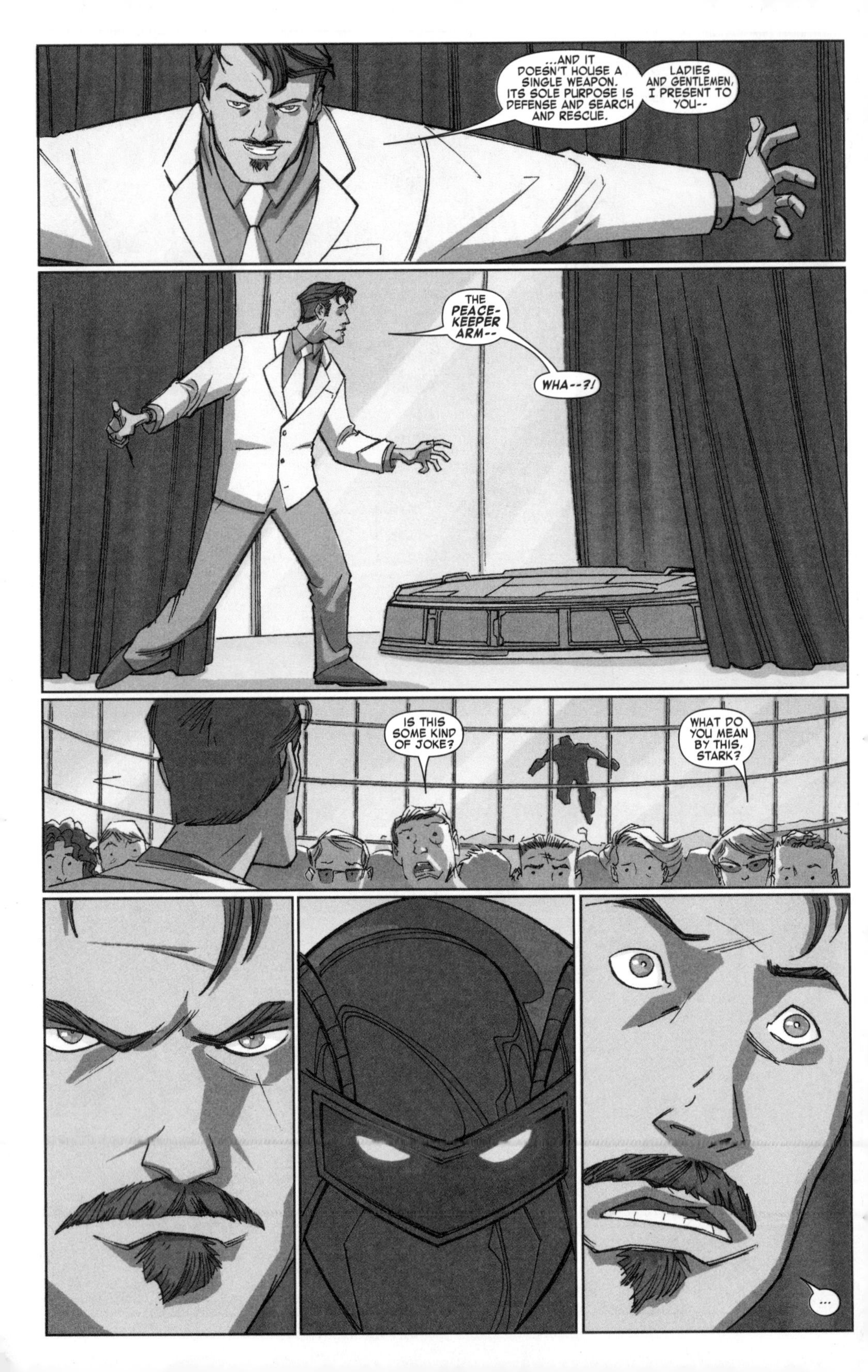
...AND IT DOESN'T HOUSE A SINGLE WEAPON. ITS SOLE PURPOSE IS DEFENSE AND SEARCH AND RESCUE.
LADIES AND GENTLEMEN, I PRESENT TO YOU--
THE PEACE-KEEPER ARM--
WHA--?!
IS THIS SOME KIND OF JOKE?
WHAT DO YOU MEAN BY THIS, STARK?
...

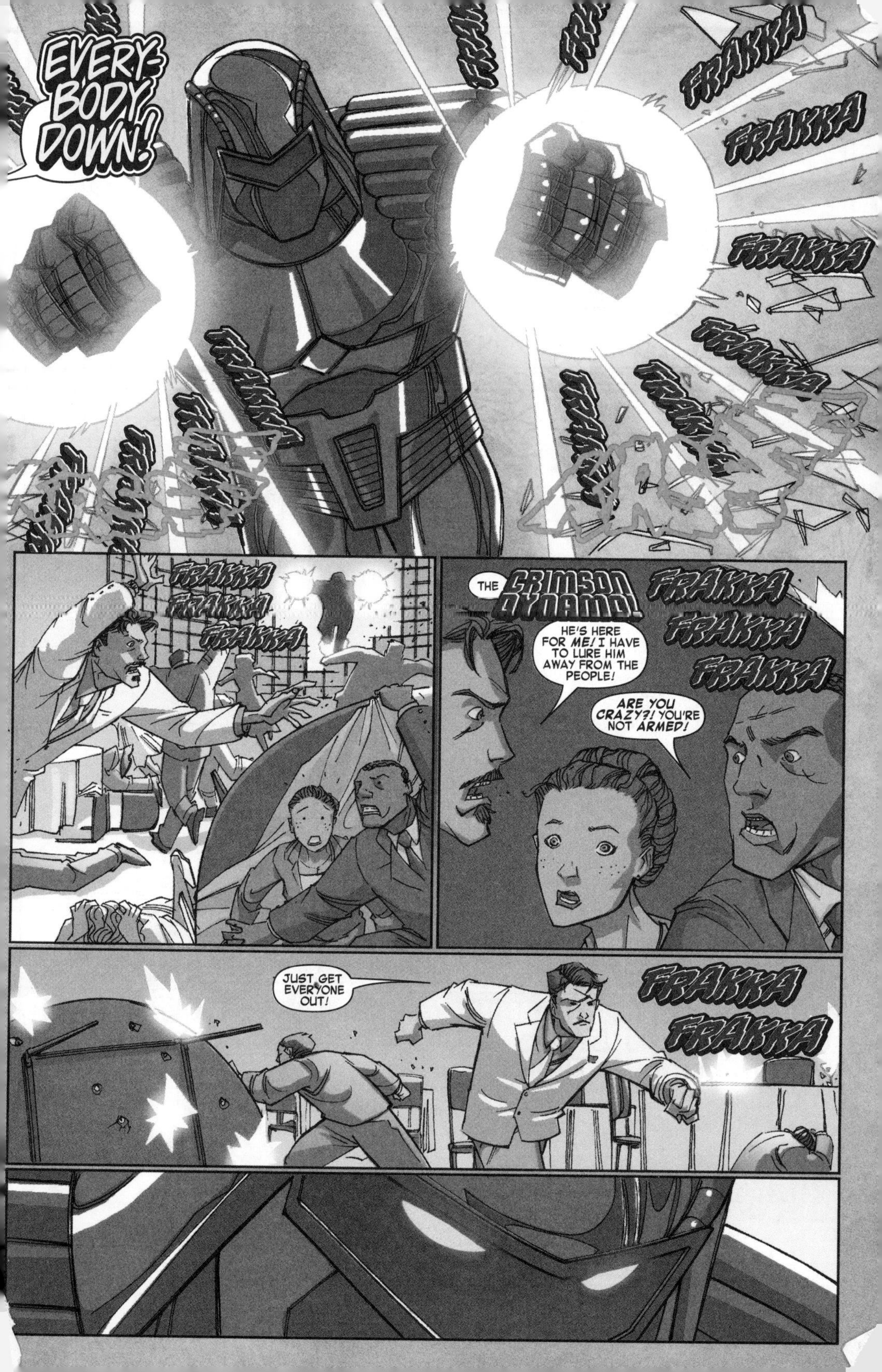
EVERY-BODY DOWN!
FRAKKA FRAKKA FRAKKA
FRAKKA
FRAKKA FRAKKA FRAKKA
THE CRIMSON DYNAMO!
FRAKKA FRAKKA FRAKKA
HE'S HERE FOR ME! I HAVE TO LURE HIM AWAY FROM THE PEOPLE!
ARE YOU CRAZY?! YOU'RE NOT ARMED!
JUST GET EVERYONE OUT!
FRAKKA FRAKKA

KSSH!
FRAKKA
KSSH
FRAKKA
KSSH!
FRAKKA
KSSH!
FRAKKA
KSSH!
KSSH!
FRAKKA
FRAKKA
KSSH!
FRAKKA FRAKKA
FRAKKA
HNNN--!
KSSH!
KSSH!
KSSH!
FIRE
FIRE
KLANGALANGALANGALANGALANG
FLOOSH

FLLLOOORSSSHHH
KLANNG!
RRRAAAGGGHHHHH!
KLUMPF
EEEEYYYYYAAAAAAAHHHH!
BBZZZZTTTTTT
HNF!
TONY!

KARRRUMMBBBLLEEE
HE'LL BE BACK ONCE HE GETS HIS BEARINGS. QUICK-- I HAVE TO GET HOME--
"--TO THE ARMORY."
I--I DON'T GET IT...
THIS IS BAD, RHODEY...
...THIS IS REEEEALLLLLLLY BAD.

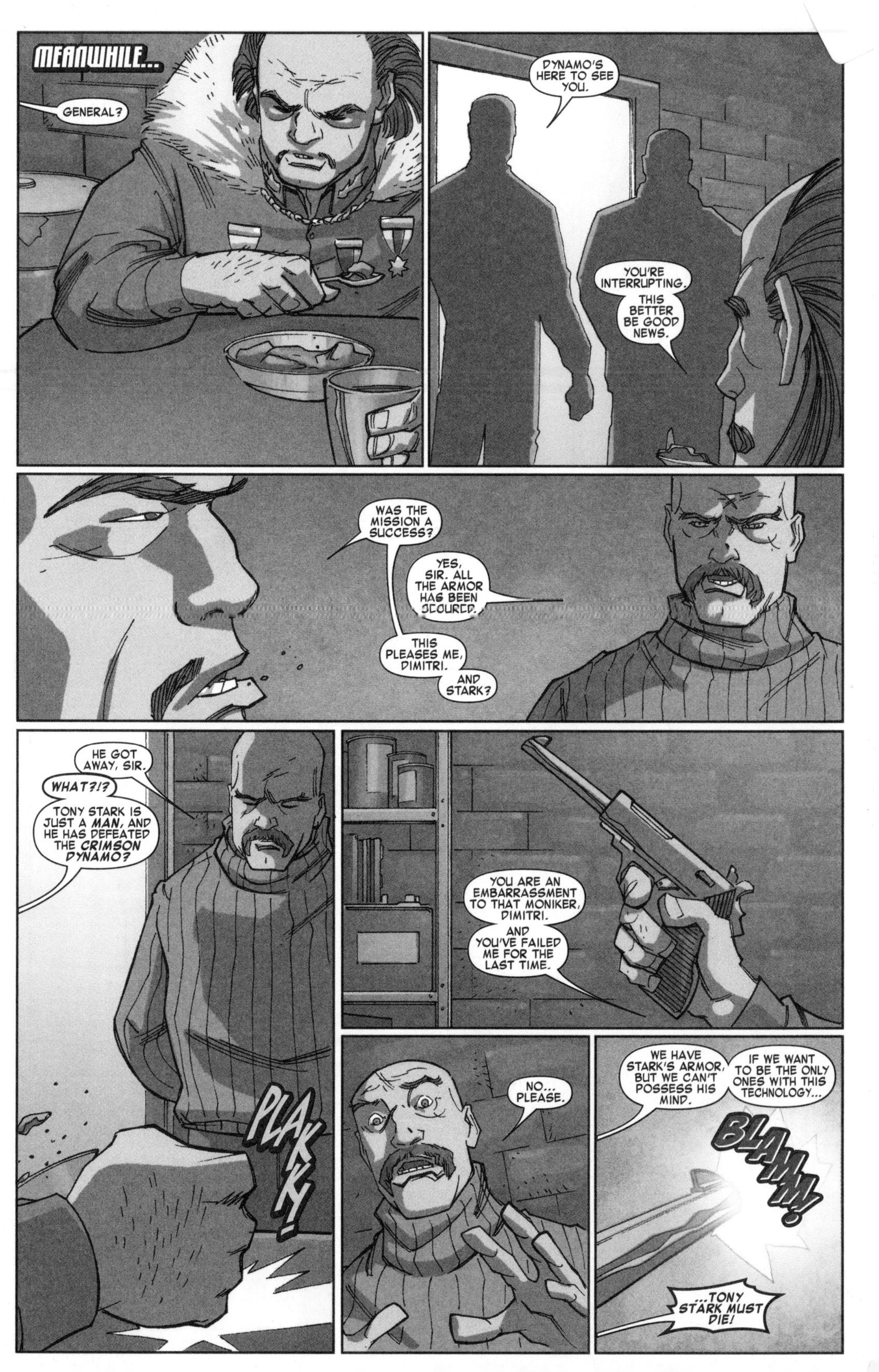
MEANWHILE...
GENERAL?
DYNAMO'S HERE TO SEE YOU.
YOU'RE INTERRUPTING. THIS BETTER BE GOOD NEWS.
WAS THE MISSION A SUCCESS?
YES, SIR. ALL THE ARMOR HAS BEEN SECURED.
THIS PLEASES ME, DIMITRI.
AND STARK?
HE GOT AWAY, SIR.
WHAT?!?
TONY STARK IS JUST A MAN, AND HE HAS DEFEATED THE CRIMSON DYNAMO?
YOU ARE AN EMBARRASSMENT TO THAT MONIKER, DIMITRI.
AND YOU'VE FAILED ME FOR THE LAST TIME.
PLAKK!
NO... PLEASE.
WE HAVE STARK'S ARMOR, BUT WE CAN'T POSSESS HIS MIND.
IF WE WANT TO BE THE ONLY ONES WITH THIS TECHNOLOGY...
BLAMM!
...TONY STARK MUST DIE!

"AND WE WILL NOT REST UNTIL HE DOES!"
YOU SLEPT IN YOUR SUIT?
PEPPER POTTS IS MY PERSONAL ASSISTANT. SHE'S GOOD PEOPLE.
SHE PROBABLY KNOWS MORE ABOUT MY BUSINESS THAN I DO.
I DIDN'T SLEEP.
OH. I CALLED--
I DIDN'T WANT TO PICK UP.
BUT THE FBI WAS HERE--
I KNOW. ANYTHING ELSE?
A LOT OF PHONE MESSAGES. MOSTLY REPORTERS, YOUR ACCOUNTANT, ONE OF YOUR ATTORNEYS... OH--
A "TIFFANY" SAYS SHE'LL BE IN TOWN NEXT WEEKEND. SHE ASKED FOR "TONY-POOH."
THROW THEM ALL AWAY.
NO, WAIT--
I'LL HOLD THIS ONE.
JUST IN CASE.
AND, UH...
...SOMEONE'S IN YOUR OFFICE.
WHERE IS THE ARMOR?!

YOU DON'T JUST LOSE A FIVE BILLION DOLLAR SUIT OF ARMOR!
I TOLD YOU, CONGRESSMAN WYNDHAM, THE CRIMSON DYNAMO--
I'M NOT INTERESTED IN ANY OF IRON MAN'S SUPER HERO MUMBO JUMBO!
MY COMMITTEE--NO, THE UNITED STATES--TRUSTED YOU, AGAINST MY BETTER JUDGMENT, WITH MONEY TO DEVELOP YOUR PRODUCT. FOR US.
YOU HAVE THE TIGHTEST SECURITY ON THE PLANET--FOR PETE'S SAKE, IRON MAN IS YOUR BODYGUARD. SO I FIND IT PECULIAR THAT SOMETHING LIKE THIS COULD EVER HAPPEN.
WHAT ARE YOU IMPLYING?
YOU EITHER WRITE A CHECK FOR FIVE BILLION, OR YOU PRODUCE THE ARMOR. TOMORROW.
THAT'S NOT POSSIBLE, CONGRESS-MAN.
I DON'T--
...
BILKING THE GOVERNMENT OUT OF BILLIONS OF DOLLARS ISN'T JUST ILLEGAL, STARK...
...IT'S TREASON!
CONGRESSMAN, DUCK!
CHERR-KLASSH!

YOU.
THAT VOICE...
...EVEN THROUGH THE HELMET...

OH, MY--
TONY!
WITHOUT MY ARMOR, I'M HELPLESS.

NO...
A STAPLER? SERIOUSLY?
WELL, I DO HAVE ONE ADVANTAGE...

KIK!
I KNOW A LOT MORE ABOUT THE SUIT THAN THE PERSON INSIDE.
PEPPER, GO!

HNNN...

AAAAH!
THERE'S A CLUSTER OF WIRES JUST UNDER THE SHOULDER PLATE.
WITH THE PROPER TOOL--
(A CUFF LINK WILL WORK IN A PINCH)
--I CAN GIVE THEM A GOOD TUG...
EXIT

EEEEEEEEEEEEEEEEEEEEEEEEEEEEEEEEEEE
AAAAAIIIIIIIIIEEEEEEEEE!!!
...AND FRY THE COMM SYSTEM.
FWARRSHHH
TWO BROKEN RIBS.
OOF!
KLUNK
AT LEAST.
MAYBE NOT THE BEST PLAN AFTER--
THAT VOICE...
IT WAS THE VOICE OF A WOMAN.
YAGGGH!

MY ARMOR... CAN'T DO THAT...

...SHE HAS... POWERS...
...BEYOND THE ARMOR'S CAPABILITIES...
...PSIONIC FROM THE...FEEL OF IT...
...THAT BLAST... RIPPED THROUGH MY BRAIN...
...LIKE A THOUSAND BABIES...CRYING AT ONCE...

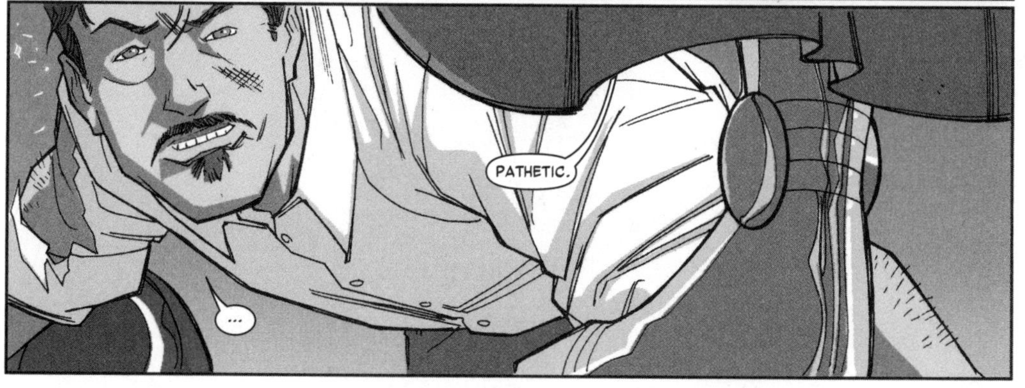
PATHETIC.
...

YOU CALL YOURSELF A HERO?

AN UNDISCLOSED UNDERGROUND LOCATION.
GENERAL!
FANTASMA'S FAILED, SIR. STARK IS STILL ALIVE!
I ASK THAT YOU KNOCK NEXT TIME, LIEUTENANT.
AND AS FOR STARK--
--HE'S PROVING TO BE MORE WORTHY AN ADVERSARY THAN I HAD ORIGINALLY THOUGHT.
WHAT DO WE DO?
FEAR NOT, STARK WILL BE DEFEATED...
"...I'M WORKING ON THAT AS WE SPEAK."
FBI
BEVERLY HILLS, CALIFORNIA...

I'M TONY STARK. A.K.A. IRON MAN.
OR, AT LEAST I WAS IRON MAN UNTIL ALL OF MY ARMOR WAS STOLEN LAST NIGHT.
NOW I'M JUST "MAN."
WHICH IS MORE THAN I CAN SAY FOR THIS THING.
YOU'RE... NOT DOOM.
VERY OBSERVANT, MR. STARK...
I AM A DOOMBOT, BUILT IN THE LIKENESS OF VICTOR VON DOOM TO ACT ON HIS BEHALF WHEN HE IS OTHERWISE OCCUPIED.
MY MASTER HAS HEARD OF YOUR LOSS...
"...AND WISHES TO OFFER HIS ASSISTANCE."
PEPPER? WHAT'S GOING ON?
JIM!
FBI
WE WERE ATTACKED--
WHAT?!
I'LL TELL YOU WHAT HAPPENED, RHODES...

...IRON MAN TRIED TO KILL ME!
EASY, CONGRESSMAN WYNDHAM.
SOMEONE IN IRON MAN ARMOR ATTACKED TONY--
--HE TORE THE PLACE TO SHREDS. I GOT EVERYONE IN THE OFFICE OUT...BUT, JIM...
DON'T LET THEM GO! THEY'RE ACCOMPLICES! THEY WORK FOR STARK!
...TONY NEVER MADE IT OUT.
"YOU WANT ME TO WHAT?"
WEAR ME.
MY BODY OPERATES INDEPENDENTLY WHEN UNOCCUPIED, BUT IS A FULLY FUNCTIONAL, WEARABLE SUIT OF DOOM ARMOR. IT HAS THE SAME CAPABILITIES AS THE ORIGINAL...
...BUT AT A FRACTION OF THE POWER, OF COURSE.
SOMETHING ABOUT THAT IS REALLY... CREEPY.
WHY WOULD DOOM WANT TO HELP ME?
THERE WILL BE TIME FOR THAT LATER...

"...RIGHT NOW, THERE ARE MANY IMPORTANT PEOPLE THAT WANT TO KNOW WHAT YOU HAVE DONE WITH THEIR MONEY...

"...WHY YOU WERE THE FIRST ONE TO LEAVE THE SCENE WHEN A HOTEL WAS BRUTALLY ATTACKED...
SWAT

"...AND WHY YOUR PERSONAL BODYGUARD ATTACKED A U.S. CONGRESSMAN."
BUT I WORK HERE!
I'M SORRY, MR. RHODES, IT'S A CRIME SCENE! I CAN'T LET YOU IN!
POLICE
BREET! BREET!

INCOMING CALL FROM: TONY

WHERE ARE YOU? ARE YOU OKAY?
RHODEY! I NEED AIR TRANSPORT RIGHT AWAY. NOT ONE OF OURS. IS THAT CLEAR?
WHAT'S HAPPENING?

MEET ME AT ANZA-BORREGO IN TWO HOURS.
WHERE ARE YOU?
LOOK UP.

IRON MAN AND THE ARMOR WARS
FWOOOOOOSH
PART 2: THE BIG RED MACHINE
"THIS IS ONE SWEET RIDE! WHERE'D YOU GET IT?"

I BORROWED IT.
JIM "RHODEY" RHODES IS MY BUSINESS ASSOCIATE, CONFIDANTE, AND BEST FRIEND...
KIND OF LIKE MY SIDEKICK, REALLY.
I DON'T KNOW ANYONE WHO OWNS ONE OF THESE...
I KNOW YOU THINK I'M JUST SOME KIND OF SIDEKICK--
SIDEKICK? I'D NEVER CALL YOU THAT!
--BUT I'M A MARINE. I'M CAPABLE OF A LOT OF THINGS THAT YOU DON'T EVEN KNOW ABOUT, TONY.
NOW, UNLESS YOU WANT TO WASTE ALL OF OUR FUEL FLYING IN CIRCLES, TELL ME WHERE WE'RE GOING.
THIS MORNING--THAT WOMAN IN IRON MAN ARMOR WHO ATTACKED ME--SHE'S A FORMER SUPREME SOVIET NAMED FANTASMA...
A RUSSIAN?
JUST LIKE CRIMSON DYNAMO.
I'M NOT SURE WHAT IT MEANS YET, BUT I KNOW THEY DIDN'T STEAL MY TECH TO TRY TO SOLVE THE ENERGY CRISIS.
OOOHHH, I GET IT. FOR ONCE IT'S NOT ABOUT YOU...IT'S A RUSSIA-U.S. THING.
RHODEY, WHEN YOU MAKE JOKES, YOU MESS WITH OUR DYNAMIC.
YOU'RE SUPPOSED TO ROLL YOUR EYES, TELL ME I'M CRAZY, AND THEN GO ALONG WITH MY PLAN ANYWAY.
WHAT IS YOUR PLAN?

NOBODY ON THE PLANET KNOWS THE TECH BETTER THAN I DO. IF I CAN STAY AWAY FROM THE FBI LONG ENOUGH, I'LL TRACK DOWN THE SUITS OF ARMOR AND DISABLE THEM ONE BY ONE.
ALL OF THEM?
YOU FORGOT TO ROLL YOUR EYES.
WATCH AND LEARN, LIEUTENANT RHODES...
I'VE MADE THOUSANDS OF ADVANCEMENTS IN MY ARMOR OVER THE YEARS, BUT THERE HAS BEEN ONE CONSTANT-- THE TONE-CODED CHANNEL I USE FOR COMMUNICATIONS.
SEE THIS? EVERY HELMET I'VE BUILT HAS A RECEIVER IN IT LIKE THIS ONE THAT'S SET TO THAT CHANNEL.
IF I JACK UP THE SIGNAL AMPLIFIER AND INCREASE THE SENSITIVITY OF THE MIC LIKE THIS, ANY COM DEVICE WITHIN FIVE HUNDRED MILES USING THE SAME CHANNEL WILL GET PICKED UP AND CREATE DISTORTION-LIKE SPEAKER FEEDBACK--
--AND THE CLOSER I GET TO IT, THE LOUDER IT'LL GET.
DID YOU JUST BUILD A SONAR... OUT OF A WALKIE-TALKIE?
YOU FLY THE PLANES, AND I BUILD MYSELF OUT OF PROBLEMS. ALSO PART OF THE DYNAMIC.
NOW LET'S SEE IF I PICK ANYTHING UP.
AND WHEN DO WE TALK ABOUT THE GIANT ELEPHANT IN THE ROOM?
YOU MEAN THE DOOM ARMOR?

YOU DON'T WANT TO KNOW.
FORT KNOX, KENTUCKY.
RATATATATATATAT
BLAM
BLAM
PING!
BLAM
BLAM
PING!
THAT'S IT! KEEP SHOOTING.
YOUR BULLETS ARE NO MATCH FOR IVAN KRUSHKI ANYMORE!
PING!
PING!
PING!
PING!
PING!
PING!
PING!
PING!
FOOLISH AMERICANS!
YYAAAHHHH!
KRUNNGGK!
EXCUSE ME.

KWAPLANG!
YOU HAVE SOMETHING THAT BELONGS TO ME.
AND SINCE I'VE GOT A FEELING THAT YOU'RE NOT THE MASTERMIND BEHIND IT ALL...
...WHEN I TEAR IT OFF OF YOU, YOU'RE GOING TO TELL ME WHO YOU'RE WORKING FO--
YOU DARE TO CHALLENGE ME?
URK!
HOW...? HOW DID I--?
I'M MORE POWERFUL THAN I THOUGHT!
OF COURSE! HE'S ONLY HAD THE SUIT FOR A DAY...
...HE DOESN'T KNOW HOW TO OPERATE IT YET.
I HAVE TO FIND A WAY TO MAKE HIM VULNERABLE.
THE OLD ARMOR'S NOT AS STURDY AS THE NEWER MODELS...

...BUT STILL EXTREMELY POWERFUL.
AND I'M AS MUCH OUT OF MY ELEMENT IN THIS DOOM ARMOR AS KRUSHKI IS IN MINE.
HE'S CRUSHING ME...
...ALREADY HARD TO BREATHE...
...WITH BROKEN RIBS...
YOU WANT TO KNOW WHO I'M WORKING FOR?
THE SAME ONE I'VE ALWAYS WORKED FOR! AND SHE'S BACK AND STRONGER THAN EVER!
I WORK FOR--
...CAN'T...
...BREATHE!
ZZRAAAKK!
I HAVE TO USE THE ARMOR AGAINST HIM.
MOTHER RUSSIAAAA AAGGGHHH!
A COUPLE OF WELL-PLACED HITS AND--

WHAT'S HAPPENED?!
I CAN'T TURN IT OFF!
FWOOOOOSH

KRUNCH

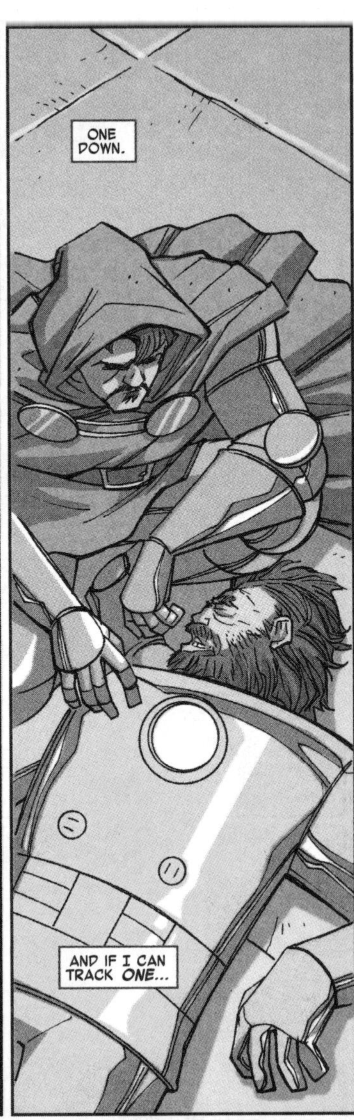
ONE DOWN.
AND IF I CAN TRACK *ONE*...

...I CAN TRACK *MORE*.
<CAPTAIN!>
DEEP BENEATH THE SEA...

<TWO BOATS APPROACHING QUICKLY, SIR!>
BLIP
BLIP
<AN ATTACK? WE WOULDN'T BE OF ANY INTEREST IN THESE WATERS... UNLESS-->
<COULD IT BE THAT SOMEONE'S FOUND OUT?>
EH?
SKRRANNCH!
PSSSSSSSSH
AAAHHH!
<OH GOD... OH GOD...>

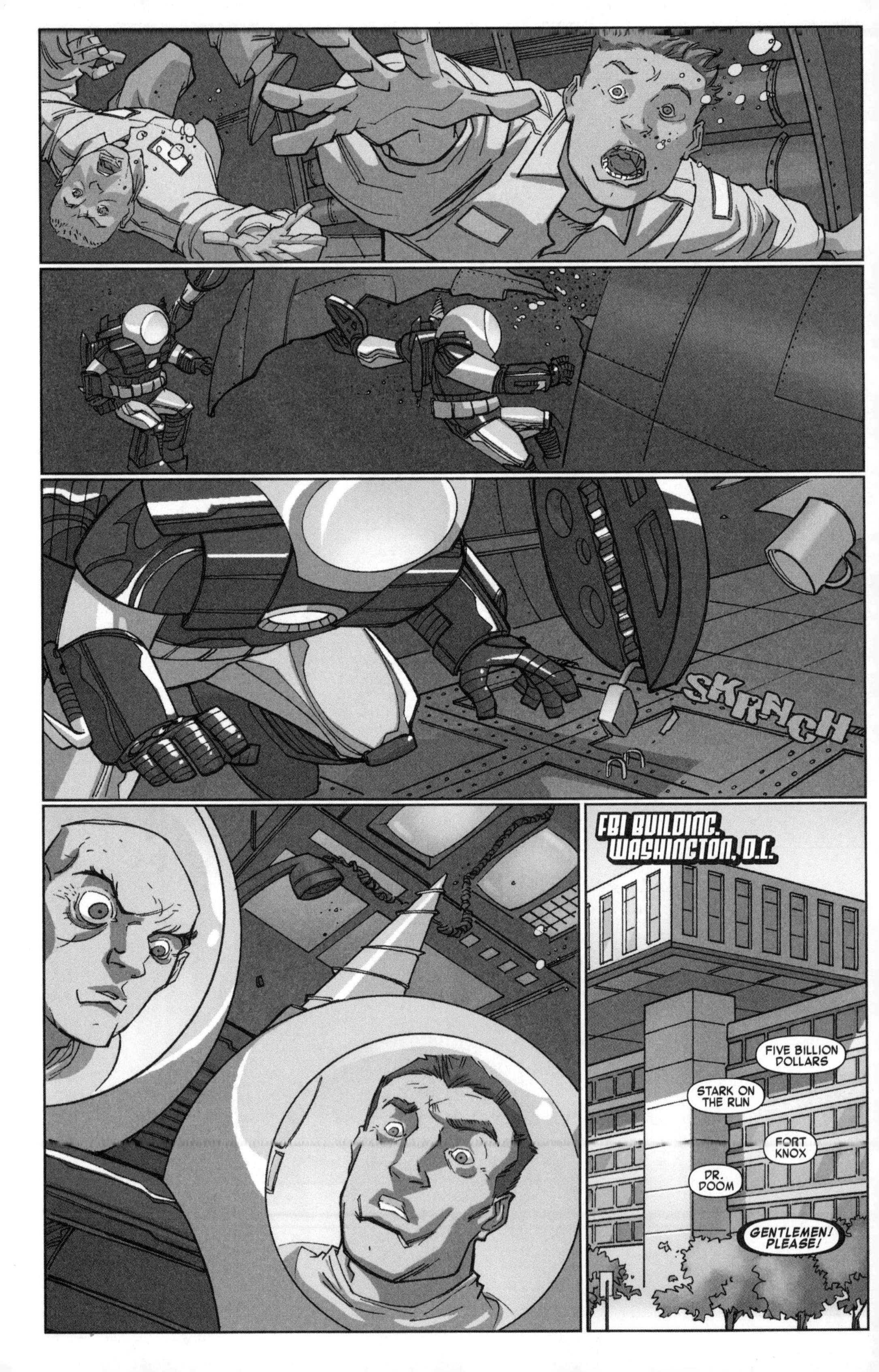
SKRNCH
FBI BUILDING.
WASHINGTON, D.C.
FIVE BILLION DOLLARS
STARK ON THE RUN
FORT KNOX
DR. DOOM
GENTLEMEN! PLEASE!

LET THE CONGRESSMAN SPEAK.
THE EVIDENCE SPEAKS FOR ITSELF, DIRECTOR STONE...
...TONY STARK IS A FUGITIVE FROM JUSTICE!
AND WITH IRON MAN AT HIS DISPOSAL, HE SHOULD BE CONSIDERED ARMED AND DANGEROUS.
WAIT A MINUTE... WE DON'T HAVE ANY REASON TO BELIEVE HE'S EVEN DONE ANYTHING WRONG.
THE WOMAN--POTTS--SHE TOLD OUR INVESTIGATORS THAT STARK WAS ATTACKED--
INNOCENT PEOPLE DON'T RUN, AGENT DEKKER.
AND WHAT ABOUT STARK'S FRIEND? JAMES RHODES. ANYTHING ON HIM?
HE LEFT THE SCENE BEFORE OUR MEN COULD QUESTION HIM.
RHODES?
HE COULD BE WITH STARK, BUT WE DON'T KNOW THAT FOR SURE.
OF COURSE HE'S WITH STARK, THEY'RE ALL IN CAHOOTS!
IF HE FLED, HE PROBABLY KNOWS SOMETHING. FINDING HIM COULD BE AS VALUABLE TO US AS FINDING STARK.
DIRECTOR, I SERVED IN THE CORPS. WITH A JAMES RHODES. COULD IT BE--?

IT SAYS HERE HE'S A FORMER MARINE.
IF IT'S THE JIM RHODES I KNOW, HE'S A PILOT. A GREAT PILOT. IF HE NEEDED TO GET FAR--
AGENT MATARI, CONTACT ALL OF THE AREA AIRPORTS--BIG AND SMALL...
...AND GET A LIST OF EVERY TAKEOFF SINCE RHODES WAS LAST SPOTTED.
CONGRESSMAN, AS YOU CAN SEE THERE'S MUCH WORK TO BE DONE. THANKS FOR THE HELP, AND WE'LL BRIEF YOU ON OUR PROGRESS WHEN YOU LAND.
DIRECTOR STONE?
IF WE FIND RHODES, I'D LIKE TO QUESTION HIM. WE HAVE...A HISTORY. HE MIGHT BE MORE WILLING TO TALK TO A FRIENDLY FACE--
BOOM
WHAT THE--?
THIS IS TOO EASY. THESE AMERICANS ARE TERRIBLY BORING.
YOU SPEAK TOO SOON, DARKSTAR...

...THEY'RE ABOUT TO MAKE IT INTERESTING!
THROW UP YOUR ARMS AND SURRENDER! THIS IS AN ORDER!
INTERESTING? THIS ARMOR MAKES US FREAKING INDESTRUCTIBLE!
SICKLE, WAIT!
THEY HAVEN'T EVEN FIRED AT US, HAMMER!
WAR'S NOT FOR THE SQUEAMISH, DARKSTAR...
SCHHNK!
...WE HAVE TO DROP THE HAMMER ON THEM...

"...BEFORE THEY DROP IT ON US!"
FWAAAA
UNN...
FEELS GOOD TO BE IN MY OWN ARMOR AGAIN.
?

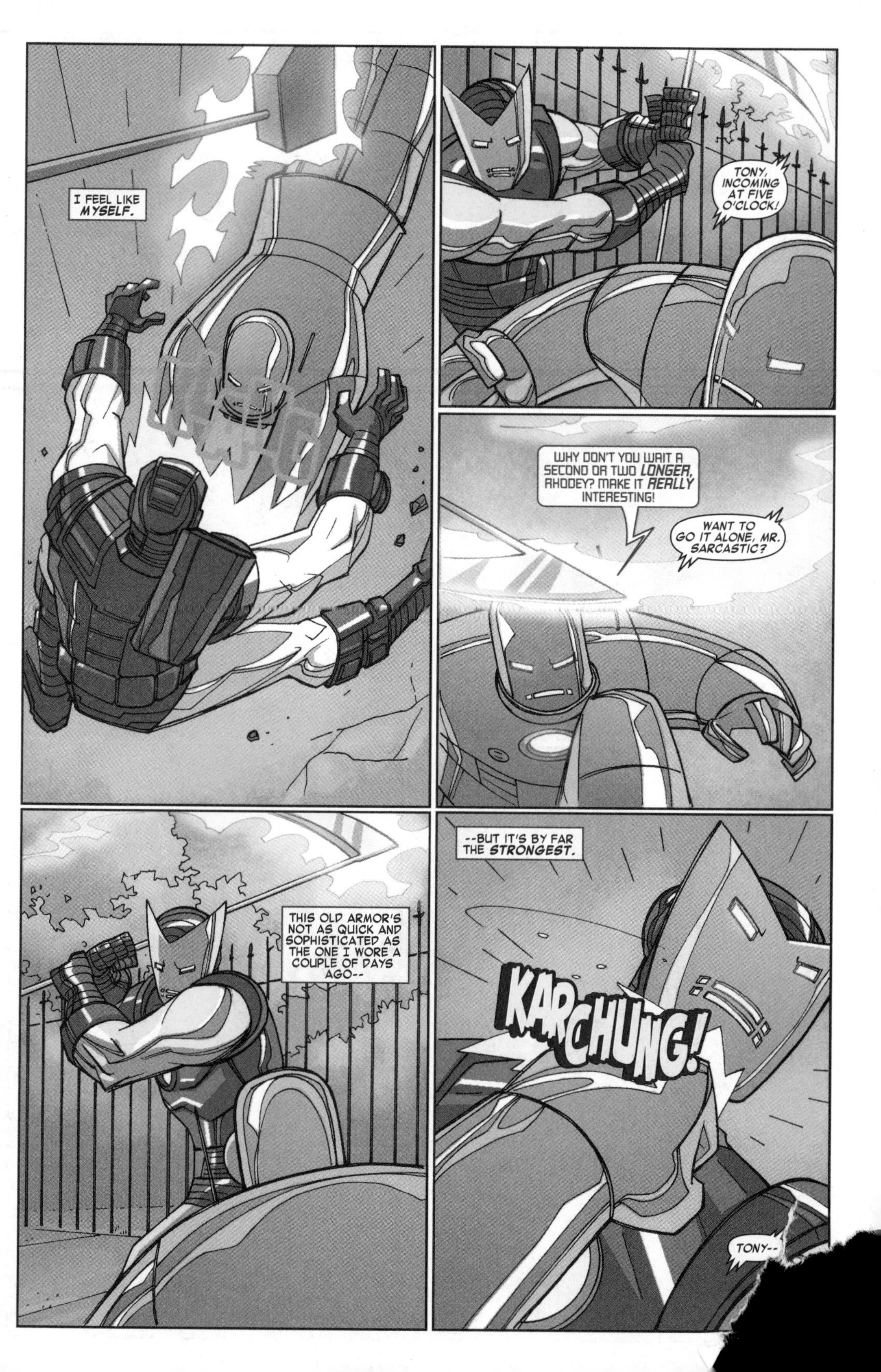
I FEEL LIKE *MYSELF.*
TONY, INCOMING AT FIVE O'CLOCK!
WHY DON'T YOU WAIT A SECOND OR TWO *LONGER,* RHODEY? MAKE IT *REALLY* INTERESTING!
WANT TO GO IT ALONE, MR. SARCASTIC?
THIS OLD ARMOR'S NOT AS QUICK AND SOPHISTICATED AS THE ONE I WORE A COUPLE OF DAYS AGO--
--BUT IT'S BY FAR THE *STRONGEST.*
KARCHUNG!
TONY--

--INCOMING AT--
--SIX O'CLOCK.
ZZZZRAKKKK!
OKAY, THAT TIME THE DELAY WORKED!
HNNN...?
YOU! STAY DOWN OR WE FIRE!
NOT WHEN YOU'RE TRAPPED IN MY DARKFORCE, YOU DON'T!
OH--!

BLA-BOOM!
CHOOM!
Y-YOU... SAVED MY LIFE!
WHY?
JUST GET OUT OF HERE.
TONE! MOVE!
NOW!
RIBS HURT SO MUCH IT'S HARD TO MOVE...I JUST BARELY GOT OUT OF THE WAY--
--BUT THE BLAST TOOK OUT THE JETS IN MY BOOTS.
HAVE TO IMPROVISE...
...NNNFFFFGGGG...

AND NOBODY IMPROVS BETTER THAN I DO.
FWOOOOSH!
UNDERGROUND.
NO NO NO NO NO NO!
GRAAAAHHH!
UM... GENERAL...?
WHY DO YOU ALL FAIL ME?
HE'S JUST ONE MAN! WE ARE A MOVEMENT!
THE FUTURE ORDER OF THE WORLD!
G-GENERAL...
YOU MISUNDERSTAND, SIR. THE OBJECT YOU REQUESTED FROM THE SUBMARINE...

...WE GOT IT.
YESSSSSSS!
YES, YES YES, YES YES!
BUT WE'RE NOT SURE EXACTLY WHAT "IT" IS.
DON'T YOU RECOGNIZE IT, URSA?

"IT'S THE GREATEST WEAPON OUR HOMELAND HAS EVER PRODUCED!"
WE HAVE TO END THIS, TONE.
WE CAN'T STOP NOW, RHODEY...
...I LET DARKSTAR GO SO WE CAN FOLLOW HER TO HER BOSS.
YOU NEED TO GET TO A HOSPITAL!
IT'S JUST A COUPLE'A BROKEN RIBS...
...AND MAYBE A SEPARATED SHOULDER... BROKEN NOSE...
I JUST NEED A FEW MINUTES TO CATCH MY BREATH AND I'LL BE FINE.
UHH...
YOU MAY NOT HAVE A FEW MINUTES...
IF YOU'VE GOT ANY MILITARY CRED AT ALL, NOW'S THE TIME, RHODEY!
REMEMBER WHEN I SAID I "BORROWED" THIS PLANE?
TECHNICALLY--
"--I STOLE IT."
FWOOSH

UNDERGROUND.
WH-WHO IS THIS, GENERAL?
A SERIAL KILLER NAMED ARKADY GREGORIVICH. FROM THE OLD COUNTRY.
A WHAT?

HE WAS SENTENCED TO EXECUTION, BUT SURVIVED.
THAT'S WHEN WE KNEW HE WAS BORN WITH CERTAIN...GIFTS, SO WE TURNED HIM OVER TO THE KGB.

THERE THEY ENHANCED THOSE GIFTS--TURNED HIM INTO A LIVING, BREATHING WEAPON. A WEAPON WE SUSPECTED THE AMERICANS COULDN'T MATCH.
UNFORTUNATELY, FOR ALL OF HIS ENHANCEMENTS, WE COULD NEVER HEAL HIS MIND.
THAT'S IT. KEEP BOTH HANDS ON HIM, URSA MAJOR. FEEL THE POWER.
THEY SAID HE WAS UNCONTROLLABLE, AND DESPITE MY PROTESTS, THEY PLACED HIM IN A CRYOGENIC FREEZE AND BURIED HIM AT THE BOTTOM OF THE SEA.
WAIT-- HE'S ALIVE?!

THAT'S WHY EVERY PIRATE IN THE WORLD WAS LOOKING FOR HIM--HE'S THE ULTIMATE BURIED TREASURE.
SO THIS RITUAL ISN'T ABOUT DRAWING HIS STRENGTH-NNGG--
NO. YOU ARE REVIVING HIM...

--BY ALLOWING HIM TO DRAW FROM YOURS.
AAARGHGGURBB...
MURDERER!

OH, DON'T WORRY. THEY'LL RECOVER...
...EVENTUALLY.
HNNNNNGH...
ERRRRRRMM...
YOU'RE A MADMAN.
I'LL EXCUSE YOUR INSUBORDINATE TONE ON ACCOUNT OF FRUSTRATION WITH YOUR FAILURES, DARKSTAR. BUT NEXT TIME...

...YOUR FATE WILL BE MORE PAINFUL AND DEFINITIVE THAN THEIRS.
IF YOU KEEP PICKING OFF YOUR OWN MEN, YOU'LL BE A LEADER WITHOUT AN ARMY, GENERAL.
BAH! YOU'VE ALL PROVEN YOURSELVES WORTH-LESS TO ME--STARK HAS STOPPED YOU AT EVERY TURN.
BUT, THANKS TO YOUR INCOMPETENCE, IT OCCURRED TO ME THAT HE MUST HAVE A WAY OF TRACKING THE ARMOR...
...SO I'M SETTING A TRAP. AND I NO LONGER NEED AN ARMY...

...I HAVE
OMEGA RED!
FINALLY, THE WESTERN WORLD WILL KNEEL TO THE NEO-SOVIETS...
...AND THE RED BARBARIAN!
HOW I LEARNED TO LOVE THE BOMB

F.B.I. HEADQUARTERS.
HIS NAME'S IVAN KRUSHKI: FORMER PROFESSIONAL WRESTLER, RUSSIAN CITIZEN.
AND HE GAVE A FULL CONFESSION?

WAS GIVEN THE IRON MAN ARMOR, WAS TOLD TO KILL TONY STARK...THE WHOLE THING.
OF COURSE, HE WAS EN ROUTE TO THE HOSPITAL WITH HEAD TRAUMA AT THE TIME, BUT THE STORY JIVES WITH WHAT WE ALREADY KNOW.
WHO ELSE KNOWS ABOUT THIS?
SO FAR? THE LOUISVILLE BRANCH AND THE TWO OF US.
GOOD. TELL *NOBODY* ELSE UNTIL WE GET A SECOND SOURCE, AGENT DEKKER.
EVEN CONGRESSMAN WYNDHAM?
ESPECIALLY CONGRESSMAN WYNDHAM.
DIRECTOR STONE!
MEN IN THE FIELD ARE IN PURSUIT OF OUR STOLEN PLANE FROM TWENTYNINE PALMS...

WE'VE *FOUND* THEM.
GET ON WITH OUR GUYS AND TELL THEM THAT, UNLESS THEY ARE UNDER ATTACK, THEY'RE TO HOLD THEIR FIRE. *YOU HEAR ME?*

"HOLD FIRE!"
FWOOOOSHHH
SOMEWHERE OVER WEST VIRGINIA.

WHAT DO YOU MEAN YOU STOLE THIS PLANE?
YOU WANTED SOMETHING UNTRACEABLE RIGHT AWAY! WHAT DID YOU EXPECT ME TO DO, CALL DIAL-A-PLANE?
I ASSUMED YOU HAD A BETTER PLAN THAN JUST FLYING AROUND AND FINDING YOUR STOLEN SUITS OF ARMOR ONE AT A TIME!
WE'VE GOT TO GET OUT OF HERE--
KRAK-KA-BOOM!
--RIGHT NOW!
BRAKKA BRAKKA BRAKKA
YAAHH!
RHODEY...MY SHOULDER...

BRAKKA
BRAKKA
BRAKKA
I'M IN PURSUIT! TARGET'S IN RANGE.

AGH! WATCH THE TREES! GET ME UP HIGHER!
I'M-- [UMPH]-- TRYING!
29% POWER REMAINING.
WHAT'S THAT?!
THE SUIT. MY OLDER MODEL TRANSISTORS... RAN ON BATTERY POWER. THEY NEED TO PLUG IN TO CHARGE.
BRAKKA
BRAKKA
BRAKKA
BRAKKA
28% POWER REMAINING.

THAT'S TICKING DOWN FAST, ISN'T IT?
THERE'S TOO MUCH DRAG ON THE POWER... I'VE GOT TO LIGHTEN MY LOAD...
HOW DO WE DO THAT?

"WE" DON'T. GRAB A TREE.
NO! I'LL KICK
YAAAHHHHHHHH--
SORRY, RHODEY...

...IF I DON'T FIND THE LOOSE SUITS, THE CONSEQUENCES ARE ON *ME!*
FWOOOOOSSSSSSHH!
I'M *IRON MAN,* A.K.A. *TONY STARK.*
MY FATHER, HOWARD, WAS THE GREATEST INVENTOR OF HIS GENERATION...
HOLD ON!
WHOA!
...SO WHEN UNCLE SAM NEEDED BIGGER AND BADDER WEAPONS FOR THE ARMS RACE WITH THE COMMIES, HE'S THE ONE THEY CALLED.
BRAKKA BRAKKA
HANG ON, CHET! I DON'T WANNA LOSE HIM!
YES, SIR. I'M STILL ON HIM--HUH?!
THE RUSSIANS COULDN'T FIND AN ANSWER TO *STARK INDUSTRIES,* AND EXHAUSTED ALL OF THEIR RESOURCES TRYING TO KEEP UP. THE BERLIN WALL CAME DOWN, AND DAD WAS A NATIONAL HERO.
KROOMPF
WHAT DO YOU MEAN, HOLD FIRE--?
SO, NATURALLY, I WANTED TO BE JUST LIKE HIM.
NO, NOT *"LIKE"* HIM...

...BETTER THAN HIM.
BY THE TIME I WAS 21, I DESIGNED ENOUGH WEAPONS ON DEFENSE CONTRACTS TO DESTROY THE WORLD FIVE TIMES OVER. BUT, AFTER THE COLD WAR, THINGS CHANGED.
PEOPLE ONLY CARED ABOUT WHERE I WAS GOING AND WHO I WAS WEARING WHILE THOSE WEAPONS SAT IN A GOVERNMENT CACHE.
OH, BELIEVE ME, I'M NOT COMPLAINING. MEN WANTED TO BE ME AND WOMEN WANTED TO BE WITH ME. I ATE IT UP.

24% POWER REMAINING.
WHEN I BUILT MY IRON MAN ARMOR--AFTER THE ACCIDENT--I WAS EVEN BIGGER. THE TABLOIDS LOVED THE ECCENTRIC RICH GUY WITH A SUPER HERO BODYGUARD. IMAGINE WHAT THEY'D DO IF THEY FOUND OUT IT WAS ACTUALLY ME IN THE ARMOR.
W-WE'RE GONNA HIT THE ROCKS!

BUT THEN, PEACETIME WAS OVER...

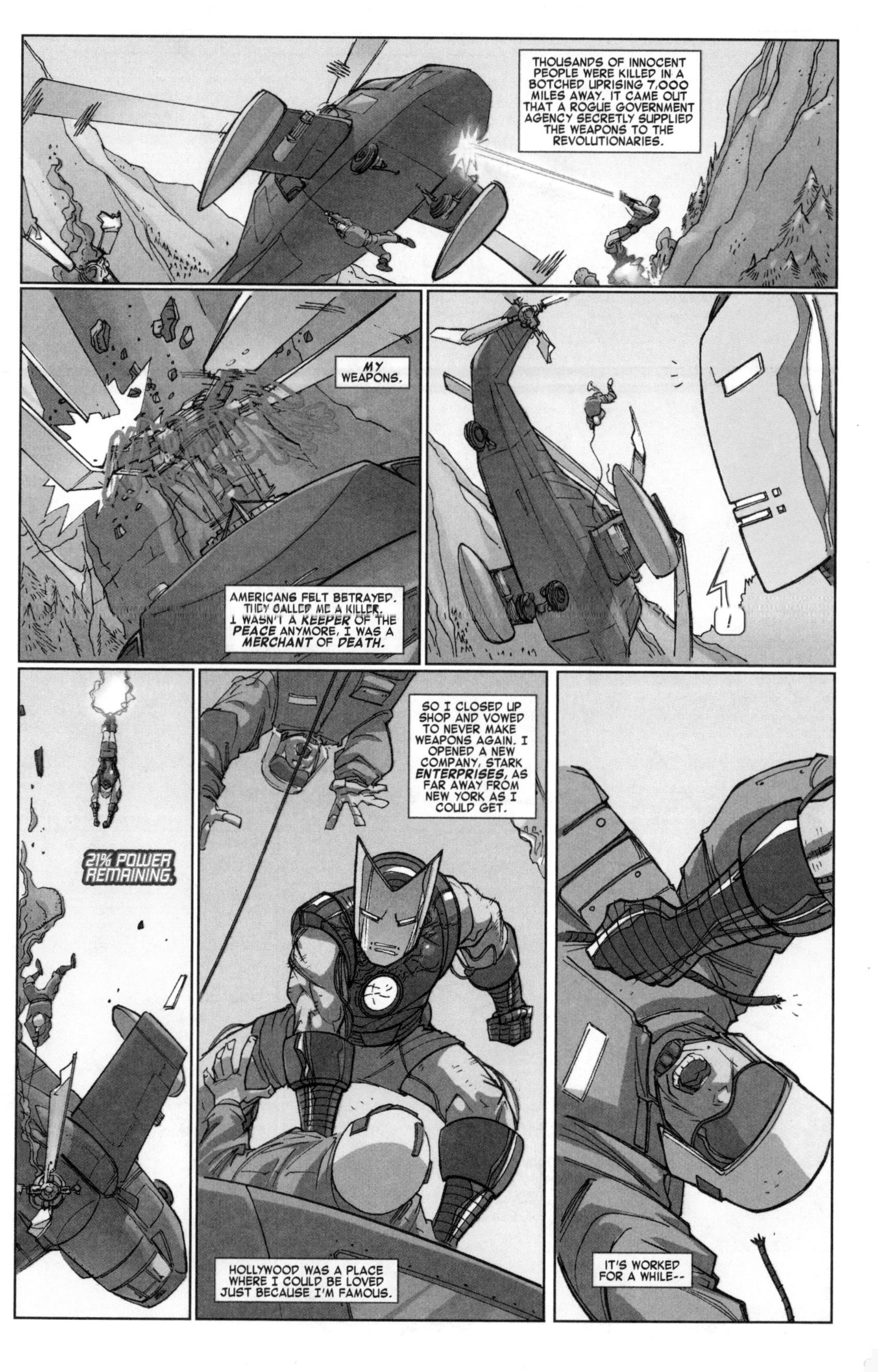
THOUSANDS OF INNOCENT PEOPLE WERE KILLED IN A BOTCHED UPRISING 7,000 MILES AWAY. IT CAME OUT THAT A ROGUE GOVERNMENT AGENCY SECRETLY SUPPLIED THE WEAPONS TO THE REVOLUTIONARIES.
MY WEAPONS.
AMERICANS FELT BETRAYED. THEY CALLED ME A KILLER. I WASN'T A KEEPER OF THE PEACE ANYMORE, I WAS A MERCHANT OF DEATH.
!
21% POWER REMAINING.
SO I CLOSED UP SHOP AND VOWED TO NEVER MAKE WEAPONS AGAIN. I OPENED A NEW COMPANY, STARK ENTERPRISES, AS FAR AWAY FROM NEW YORK AS I COULD GET.
HOLLYWOOD WAS A PLACE WHERE I COULD BE LOVED JUST BECAUSE I'M FAMOUS.
IT'S WORKED FOR A WHILE--

--UNTIL ALL OF MY IRON MAN ARMORS WERE STOLEN, AND LIFE GAVE ME ANOTHER KICK IN THE SEAT CUSHION.
EEEEEEEEEEEEEEEEEEEEEEEE
19% POWER REMAINING.
EEEEEEEL
THAT OBNOXIOUS NOISE IS MY DO-IT-YOURSELF SONAR THAT I BUILT TO TRACK THE STOLEN ARMOR.
I MUST BE STANDING ON A *BUTT-LOAD* OF THEM.
EEEEEEEL
CHET, ARE YOU OKAY?
YEAH...

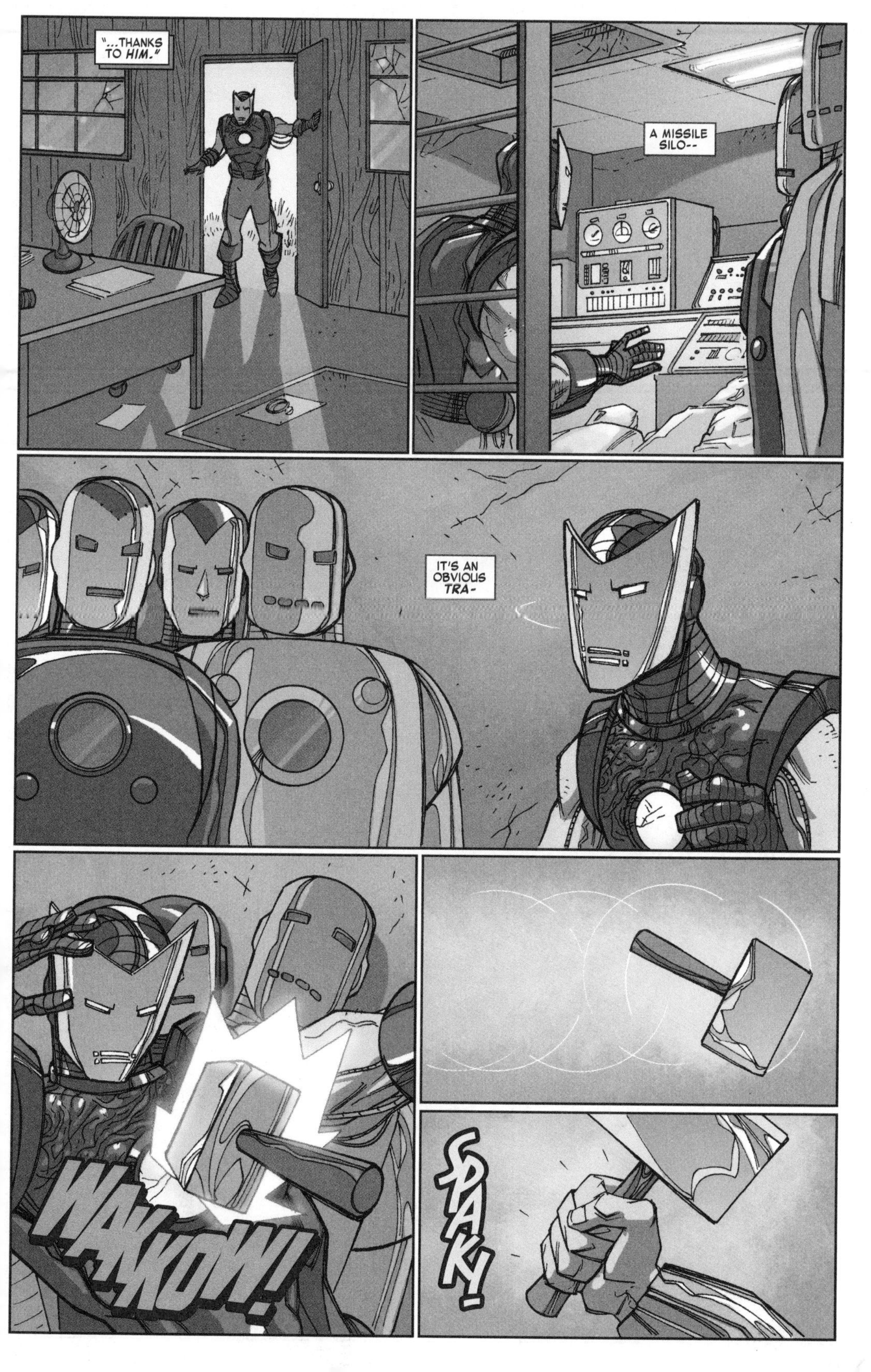
"...THANKS TO *HIM*."
A MISSILE SILO--
IT'S AN OBVIOUS *TRA-*
WAKOW!
SPAK!

VANGUARD.
HA! YOU HAVEN'T FORGOTTEN ABOUT MY FORCE FIELD, HAVE YOU, IRON MAN?
I KNOW YOU HAVEN'T FORGOTTEN THE HAMMER AND SICKLE. YOU STARKS ARE VERY FAMILIAR WITH THOSE.
AAAAAAAGH!
GRAAAH--
--AAAHHH!
THWOOSH
YOU HAVEN'T FORGOTTEN MY BOOTS' JETS, HAVE YOU?
16% POWER REMAINING.
IN YOUR DEFENSE, YOU'RE NOT USUALLY TASTING THEM.
*
TWO OF THEM...

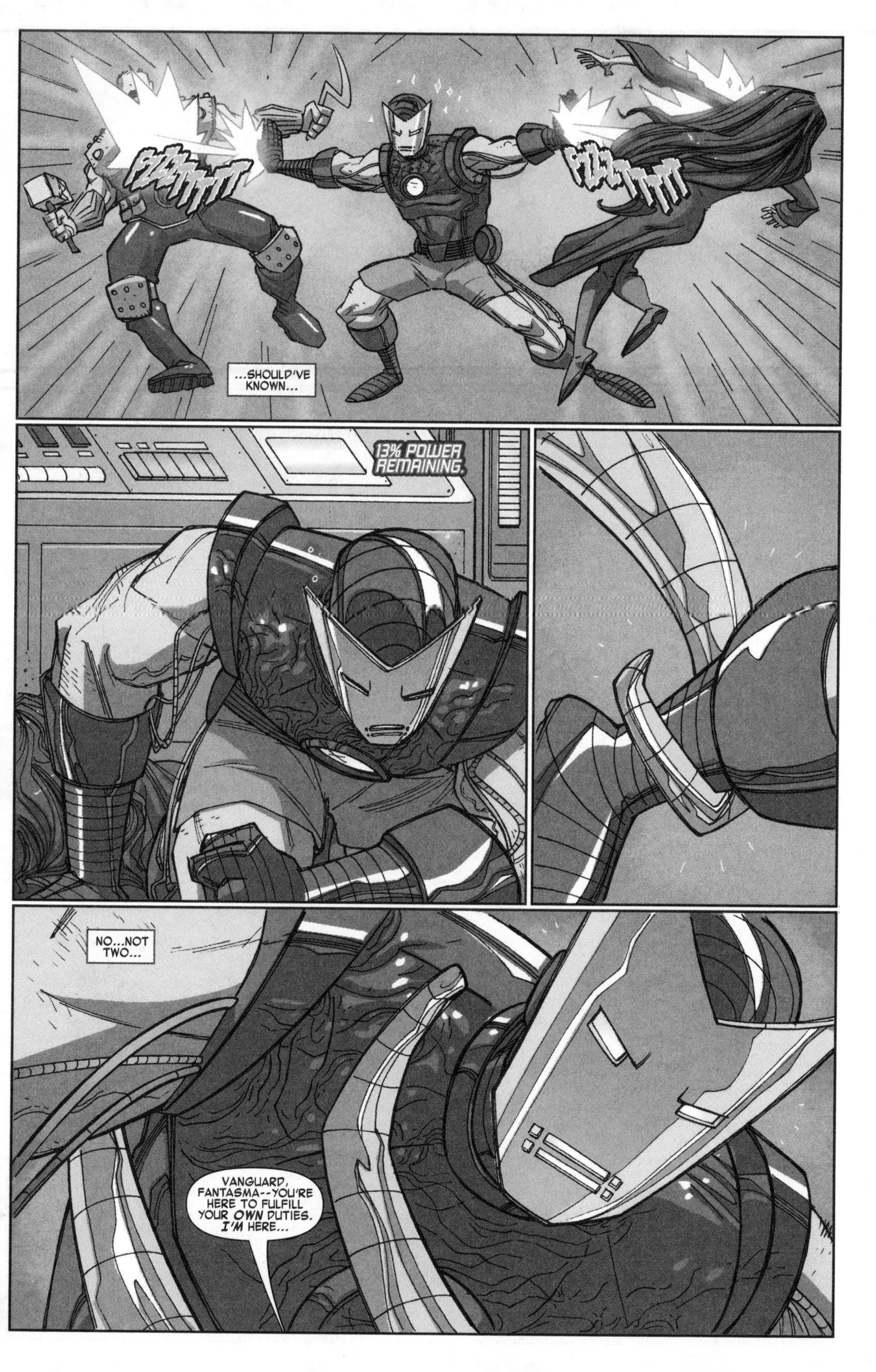
FZZZTTTTT
FZZZTTTTT
...SHOULD'VE KNOWN...
13% POWER REMAINING.
NO...NOT TWO...
VANGUARD, FANTASMA--YOU'RE HERE TO FULFILL YOUR OWN DUTIES. I'M HERE...

...THREE OF THEM.
...TO COLLECT THE SPOILS OF MY LIFE'S MISSION--
WH-WHAT...IS THIS THING?
KA-RUNCH!
BZZT!
BZZT!

THE BLOOD OF A STARK!
LAUNCH SEQUENCE INITIATED.
LAUNCH? OH, NO...
I HAVE TO END THIS. BUT HE'S AS STRONG AS THE *THING*--IN *THIS* CONDITION, AND WITHOUT THE STRENGTH OF MY FULL ARMOR...

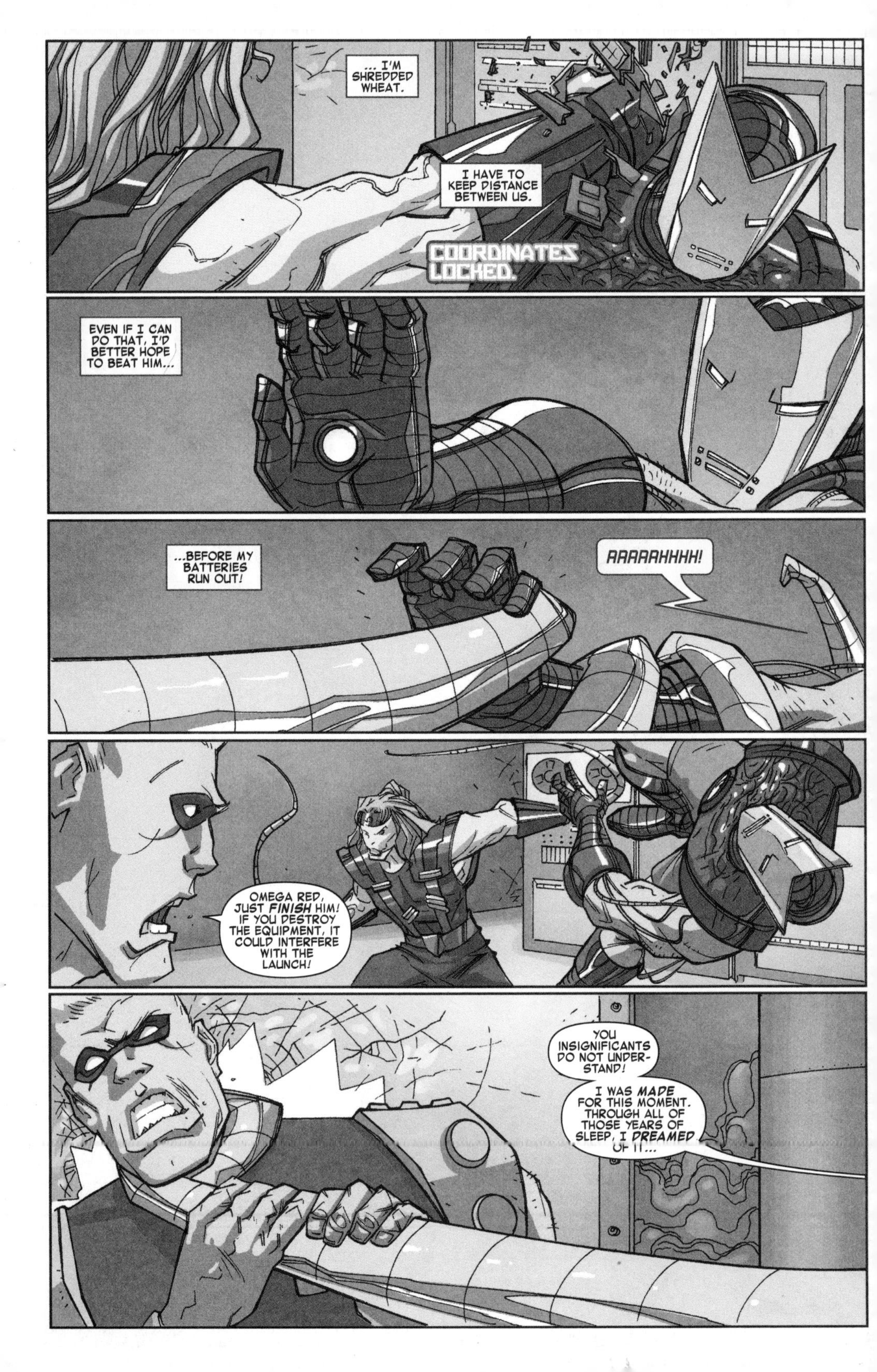
... I'M SHREDDED WHEAT.
I HAVE TO KEEP DISTANCE BETWEEN US.
COORDINATES LOCKED.
EVEN IF I CAN DO THAT, I'D BETTER HOPE TO BEAT HIM...
...BEFORE MY BATTERIES RUN OUT!
AAAAAHHHH!
OMEGA RED, JUST FINISH HIM! IF YOU DESTROY THE EQUIPMENT, IT COULD INTERFERE WITH THE LAUNCH!
YOU INSIGNIFICANTS DO NOT UNDER-STAND!
I WAS MADE FOR THIS MOMENT. THROUGH ALL OF THOSE YEARS OF SLEEP, I DREAMED OF IT...

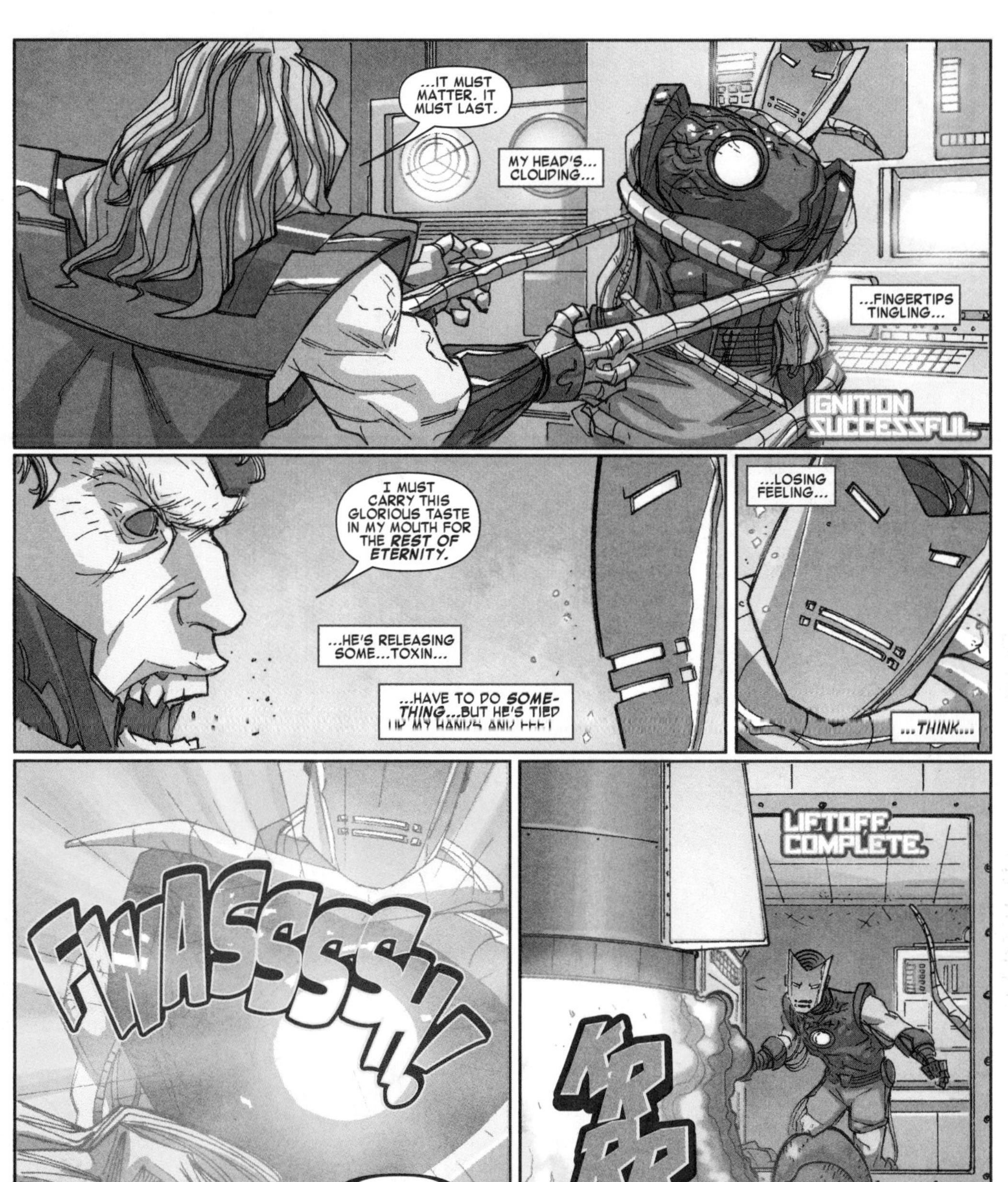
...IT MUST MATTER. IT MUST LAST.
MY HEAD'S... CLOUDING...
...FINGERTIPS TINGLING...
IGNITION SUCCESSFUL.
I MUST CARRY THIS GLORIOUS TASTE IN MY MOUTH FOR THE *REST OF ETERNITY.*
...HE'S RELEASING SOME...TOXIN...
...HAVE TO DO *SOME-THING*...BUT HE'S TIED
...LOSING FEELING...
...*THINK*...

FWASSSSH!
GRAH!

LIFTOFF COMPLETE.
KRRRRROOOOOOM!

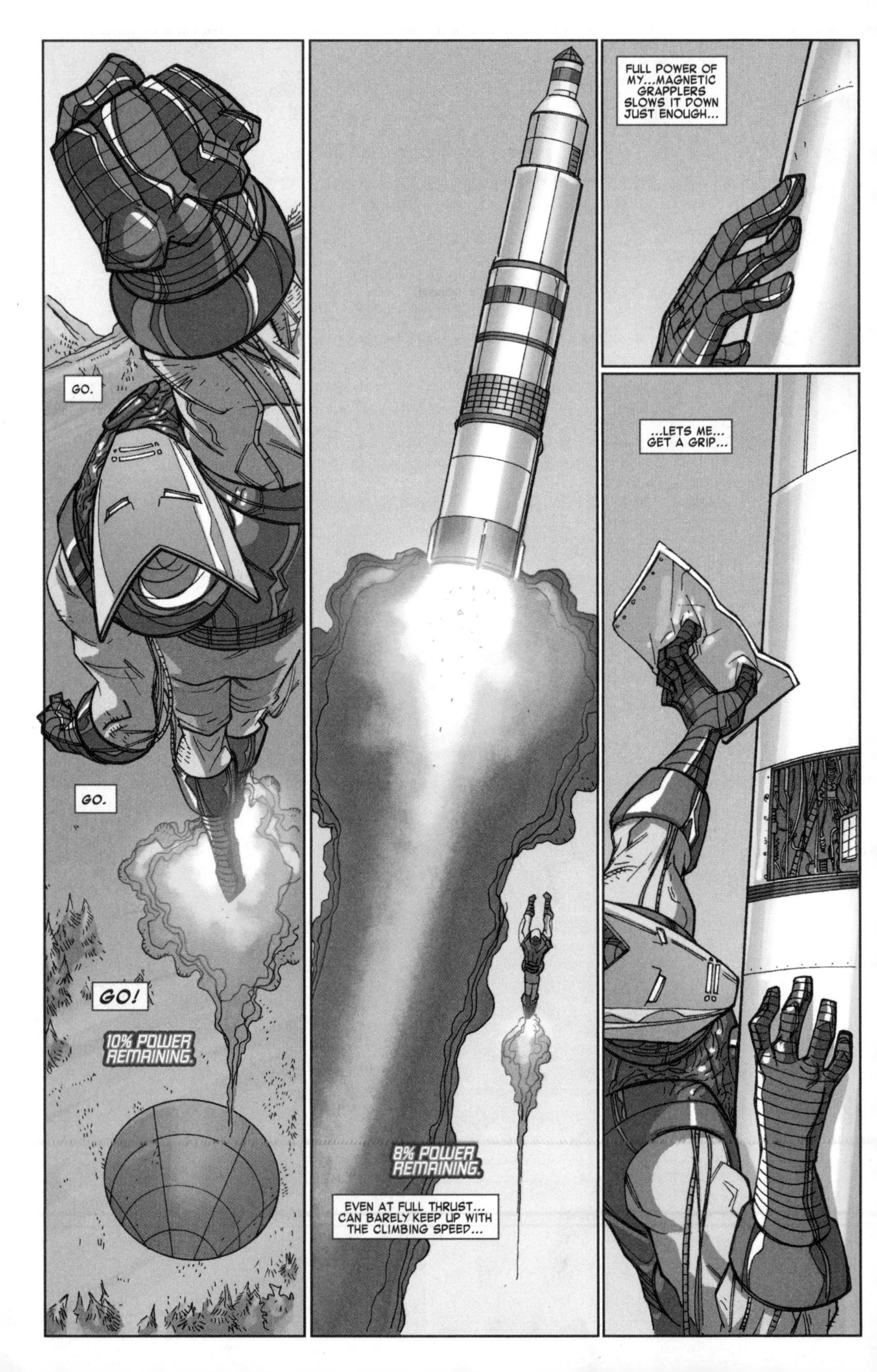
GO.
GO.
GO!
10% POWER REMAINING.
8% POWER REMAINING.
EVEN AT FULL THRUST... CAN BARELY KEEP UP WITH THE CLIMBING SPEED...
FULL POWER OF MY...MAGNETIC GRAPPLERS SLOWS IT DOWN JUST ENOUGH...
...LETS ME... GET A GRIP...

...SO I CAN DISABLE THE TRACKING SYSTEM...
STARK

BUT IT'S STILL GOING, ON A COURSE TO NOWHERE.
HAVE TO STEER IT AWAY FROM THE GROUND... UP TOWARDS SPACE...

COME ON...
4% POWER REMAINING.

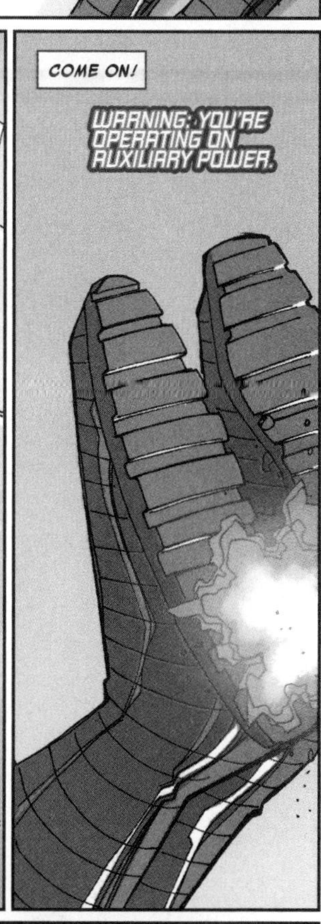
COME ON!
WARNING: YOU'RE OPERATING ON AUXILIARY POWER.

THAT'S IT...
...THIS IS MY LAST SHOT...

KRAKKA-DOOOOM
POWERING DOWN.
GOOD DAY, MR. STARK.
SPLOOSH!

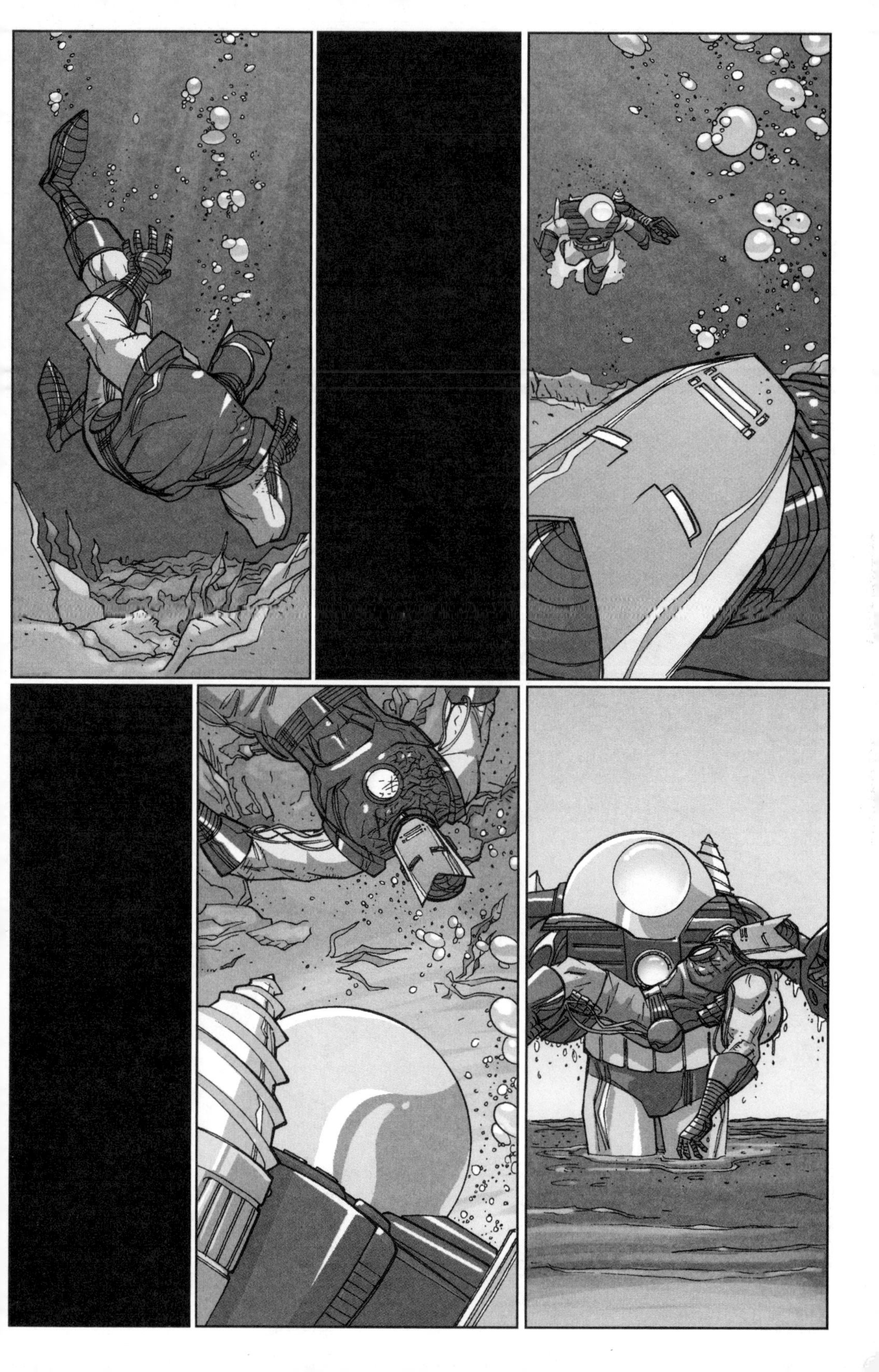

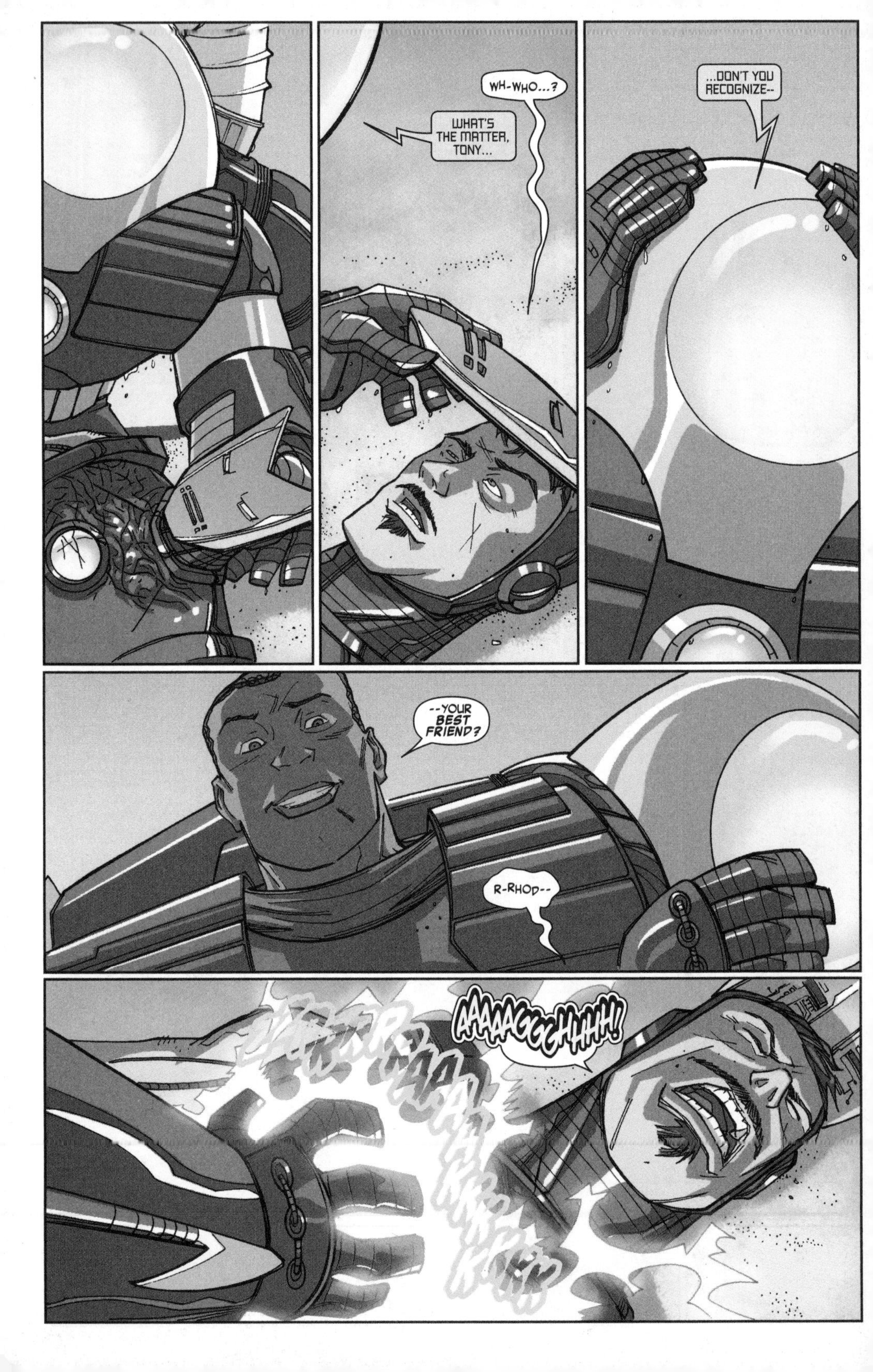
WHAT'S THE MATTER, TONY...
WH-WHO...?
...DON'T YOU RECOGNIZE--
--YOUR BEST FRIEND?
R-RHOD--
AAAAAGGGHHHH!

WAKE UP, MR. STARK.

HNNNH...

I'M TONY STARK, A.K.A. ***IRON MAN.***

SOME PEOPLE SAY I'M A PLAYBOY.

THEY SAY IT LIKE IT'S A BAD THING, BUT I THINK IT'S A VIRTUE.

BECAUSE WHEN YOU HAVE ATTACHMENTS TO PEOPLE...

...SINCE YOU WILL NOW BE WORKING FOR ME.
YOU'RE NOT GOING TO KILL ME NOW THAT YOU HAVE THE CHANCE? YOU REALLY ARE CRAZY.
YOU'RE A BUSINESSMAN, MR. STARK. YOU KNOW HOW TERRIBLY SHORTSIGHTED THAT WOULD BE. YOUR LIFE WILL BE SPARED...
...IF YOU BECOME THE WEAPONS ENGINEER FOR MY NEO-SOVIETS.
HEH HEH.
HA HA HA!
WHAT IS SO FUNNY?
HAHA...YOU MEAN TO TELL ME...HAHA...
...THE ONLY THING YOU SOVIETS COULD COME UP WITH AFTER ALL THESE YEARS...
...IS THE ONLY WAY YOU CAN WIN IS WITH AMERICAN INGENUITY?!
HA HA HA!
KRAK!

BACK IN THE DAY, RED BARBARIAN RAN A SPY RING FOR THE SOVIETS, SO IT'S NO SURPRISE HE WAS ABLE TO INFILTRATE STARK ENTERPRISES AND STEAL ALL OF MY IRON MAN ARMOR...
I'M SORRY I LOST MY MANNERS, MR. STARK, BUT I'D APPRECIATE SOME RESPECT.
WE'LL LEAVE YOU TO DECIDE YOUR FATE--JOIN US OR DIE.
OMEGA RED... COME!
...I JUST NEVER THOUGHT ANY-ONE COULD GET TO RHODEY.
WHAT IS HE THINKING? AFTER EVERYTHING I'VE DONE FOR HI--
WOW. SHE TOTALLY WANTS ME.
MEANWHILE...
MICHELINIE FEDERAL CORRECTIONS INSTITUTION, CUMBERLAND, MARYLAND.
WHY DIDN'T YOU CALL US SOONER?
I WAS OPERATING UNDER THE ORDERS OF CONGRESSMAN WYNDHAM, SIR.
WYNDHAM?!

YOU'VE CROSSED THE LINE, CONGRESSMAN-- INTERFERING WITH A FEDERAL INVESTIGATION!
I'M DOING WHAT'S BEST FOR MY COUNTRY, DIRECTOR STONE!
YOU'RE SOFT ON STARK, DIRECTOR STONE. IF I DON'T INTERVENE, WE'LL NEVER BRING HIM IN.
OH, REALLY?
PERHAPS IT'D BE BEST FOR THE COUNTRY TO KNOW THE REASON YOU HAVE A MAD-ON FOR STARK ENTERPRISES IS BECAUSE YOU'VE BEEN TAKING ILLEGAL CAMPAIGN CONTRIBUTIONS FROM HAMMER INDUSTRIES FOR YEARS.
...
I'M THE FBI DIRECTOR, CONGRESSMAN. I HAVE FILES ON EVERYONE.
AGENT DEKKER? GO DO YOUR THING.
YES, SIR.
YOU AND I WILL TALK ABOUT THIS LATER, CONGRESSMAN...
WILL YOU BE HOME OR WITH YOUR MISTRESS?
GULP!
KEITH DEKKER?

THE GOLDEN AVENGER STRIKES BACK
JAMES RHODES.
IT'S GOOD TOO SEE YOU, BUDDY.
YOU'RE WITH THE FBI.

YOU'RE STEALING MILITARY AIRCRAFT.
TO EACH HIS OWN.
BUT I'LL SAVE YOU A LOT OF WORK AND TELL YOU WHAT I TOLD YOUR BUDDIES--I DID THE CRIME, SO I'LL DO THE TIME.
WELL, THAT'S NOT *EXACTLY* WHY I'M HERE.
WHERE IS TONY STARK?

OUR GUYS SAW YOU AND IRON MAN ESCAPE FROM THE PLANE BEFORE IT WENT DOWN, BUT STARK WAS NOWHERE IN SIGHT.
YOU DON'T UNDERSTAND, JIM...
YOU KNOW I'D NEVER RAT ON A FRIEND, DEKKER.
...WE GOT A CONFESSION FROM ONE OF THE GUYS IN CUSTODY, IVAN KRUSHKI. IF HIS DETAILS ARE TRUE, STARK'S THE TARGET OF A GROUP CALLED THE NEO-SOVIETS.
WE THINK THEY'RE LOCATED SOMEWHERE IN NEW YORK, BUT HE'S A LOW-LEVEL GUY. HE WASN'T PRIVY TO THE LOCATION.
WE'RE NOT AFTER STARK, WE'RE TRYING TO *SAVE* HIM.
WHY SHOULD I BELIEVE YOU?
DO YOU REMEMBER DESERT STORM, JIM? REMEMBER KHAFJI?
YOU *KNOW* I DO. WE LOST A LOT OF BROTHERS THAT DAY. YOU WOULD HAVE BEEN ONE OF THEM--
--IF NOT FOR *YOU*.
I *CAN'T* LIE TO YOU. I *OWE* YOU THE TRUTH.
HM.
WELL, I DON'T KNOW WHERE HE IS. WE GOT SEPARATED...
...BUT IF ANY OF THE GUYS YOU PICKED UP HAD AN IRON MAN HELMET ON, TONY TAUGHT ME HOW TO *TRACK* HIM.
"YOU SAID THAT STARK WAS *MINE!*"

I WANT HIS BLOOD! NOW!
GRAAAAHHHHHHHH!!!
ARGH! WHAT'S HAPPENING TO ME?!
G-GENERAL--?!
DON'T LOSE YOUR NERVE, LIEUTENANT. THE KGB INDOCTRINATED HIM WITH A ONE-TRACK MIND, BUT IN CASE HE REALLY LOSES IT, I SET ASIDE ONE OF STARK'S CREATIONS FOR MY OWN USE.
THAT WAS WHEN CAPTURING HIM WAS AN IMPOSSIBILITY, ARKADY. WE HAVE THE IRON MAN ARMOR TO OVERTHROW THIS NATION, BUT WITH A LIMITLESS SUPPLY, WE CAN CONTROL IT.
HE'S TOO VALUABLE AN ASSET, IF HE CAN BE TURNED.
ARKADY...
...THE CARBONADIUM OF YOUR COILS IS TOXIC TO YOUR BLOOD. IT MAKES YOU...UNSTABLE. YOU JUST NEED TO FEED ON A LIFE FORCE AND YOU'LL BE BETTER.
YOU'VE BEEN PROGRAMMED TO CRAVE THE LIFE OF A STARK, BUT IT COULD BE ANYONE'S. FIGHT YOUR URGES. TAKE SOMEONE ELSE'S--
ULP!
I CANNOT WAIT ON YOU ANY LONGER!
!
FWAK!

HNNNFFFF...
CHK
CHK

WHO'S--?
OH, DARKSTAR. IT'S YOU.
AH, I GET IT-- WHAT FUN IS IT TO THROW YOURSELF AT ME IF MY HANDS ARE TIED, EH?
I'M NOT LOOKING FOR ROMANCE, YOU IDIOT!
THEN WHAT--?
THE GENERAL'S GONE MAD. WHEN HE ASKED ME TO JOIN THE NEO-SOVIETS, I THOUGHT IT WAS FOR A NOBLE CAUSE--
--BUT IT'S BECOME AN OBSESSION. HE'S DETERMINED TO WIN AT ALL COSTS, EVEN IF IT'S OUR OWN LIVES.
IT'S A SUICIDE MISSION THAT HAS TO BE STOPPED. BESIDES...
...YOU SAVED MY LIFE. IT'S MY HONOR TO SAVE YOURS.
STARK!

THROKKKKK!
THE TIME IS LONG OVERDUE...
...FOR ME TO FULFILL MY DESTINY...
...AND YOURS.
AND THIS TIME I WILL SHOW NO MERCY--
EH?
TRY AS YOU MIGHT, WOMAN, YOU CANNOT STOP THE INEVITABLE...

...STARK DIES TODAAAYYYY!
JEEZ, THIS GUY NEVER SHUTS UP.
WHERE CAN I FIND THE REST OF THIS ARMOR?
MOMENTS LATER...
HNNNH...

YOU.
HOW LONG HAS THIS BEEN GOING ON, RHODEY? MONTHS? YEARS?
WERE YOU EVER REALLY MY FRIEND AT ALL? WAS THIS YOUR PLAN SINCE DAY ONE?
I TRUSTED YOU WITH MY SECRETS. INVITED YOU INTO MY HOME.
TONY--MR. STARK--YOU DON'T UNDERSTAND--
AND THIS IS HOW YOU REPAY ME?!
BY MAKING A FOOL OUT OF ME?!
SPATTT
STARK! HE'S--

NOT RHODEY...?
WE CALL HIM THE ACTOR.
HE CAN SCULPT HIS FACE TO LOOK LIKE ANYONE'S. AND HIS POWERS OF MIMICRY ARE UNCANNY. HE'S THE GENERAL'S NUMBER ONE SPY.
I'VE BEEN TIGHT WITH RHODEY FOR YEARS...
...HOW COULD I NOT HAVE KNOWN?
TEK
LET'S GET THE BARBARIAN.
GENERAL?
KRAARRUNNCH!

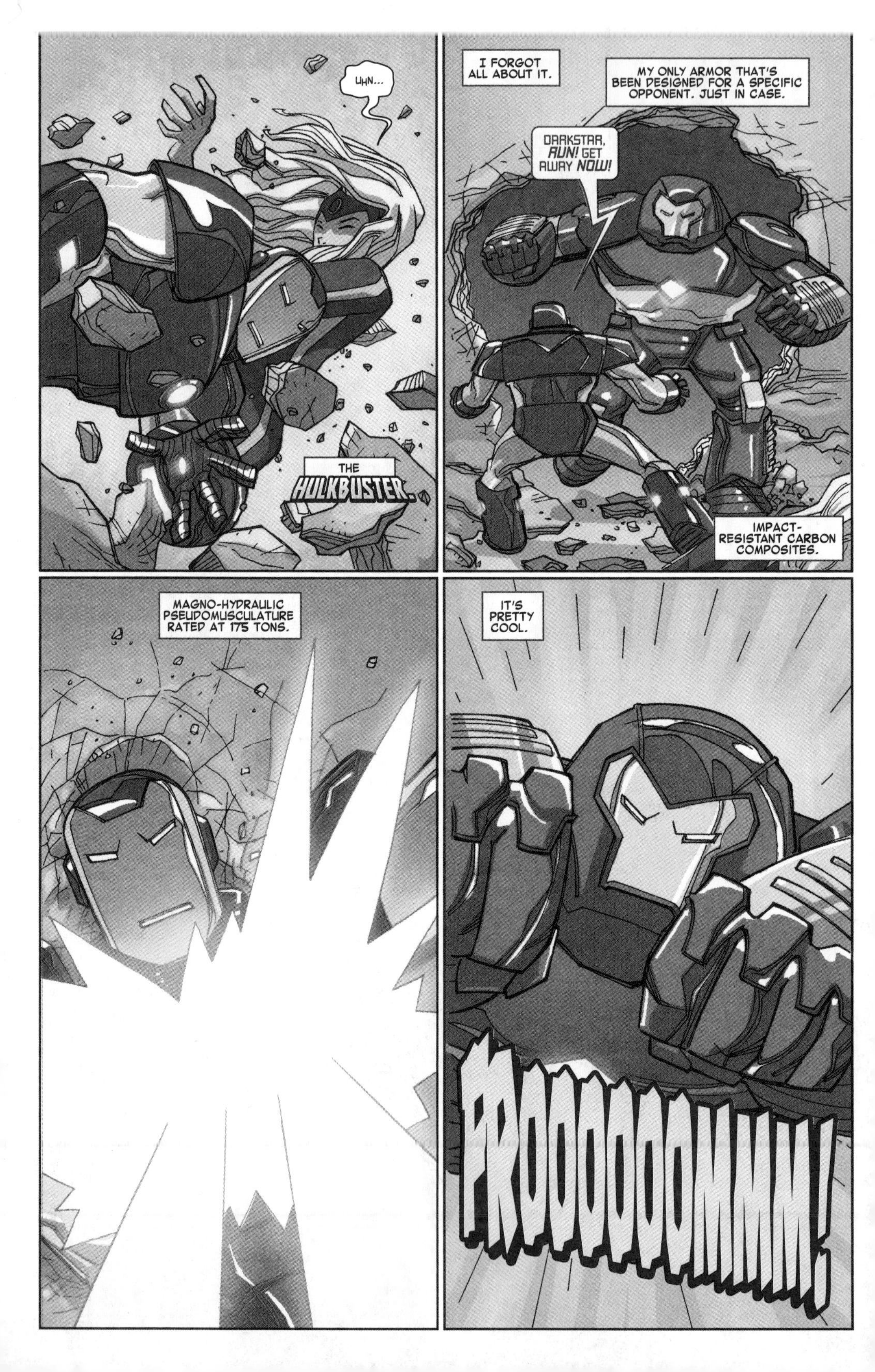
UHN...
THE HULKBUSTER.
I FORGOT ALL ABOUT IT.
MY ONLY ARMOR THAT'S BEEN DESIGNED FOR A SPECIFIC OPPONENT. JUST IN CASE.
DARKSTAR, RUN! GET AWAY NOW!
IMPACT-RESISTANT CARBON COMPOSITES.
MAGNO-HYDRAULIC PSEUDOMUSCULATURE RATED AT 175 TONS.
IT'S PRETTY COOL.
FROOOOOOMMMM!

OW.
IT'S OVER, BARBARIAN. YOU'RE BEATEN. WE DON'T NEED TO DO THIS!
THESE PEOPLE--!
YOU FOOL!
KRAKKLLLE
?!
THESE PEOPLE DON'T FEAR ME, THEY FEAR YOU!

THE AMERICAN WAY IS IMPERIALISM--
THE ELITE PROFITING ON THE BACKS OF THE WORKING CLASS.
AND YOU ARE THE WORST OFFENDER!
OOOF!
WATCH THAT THIRD RAIL, TONY. TWO HUNDRED POUNDS OF METAL AND ENOUGH ELECTRICITY TO POWER THE SUBWAY SYSTEM ISN'T A GOOD MIX.

OH--

DON'T WORRY, YOU'RE SAFE.
JUST GO. QUICKLY.

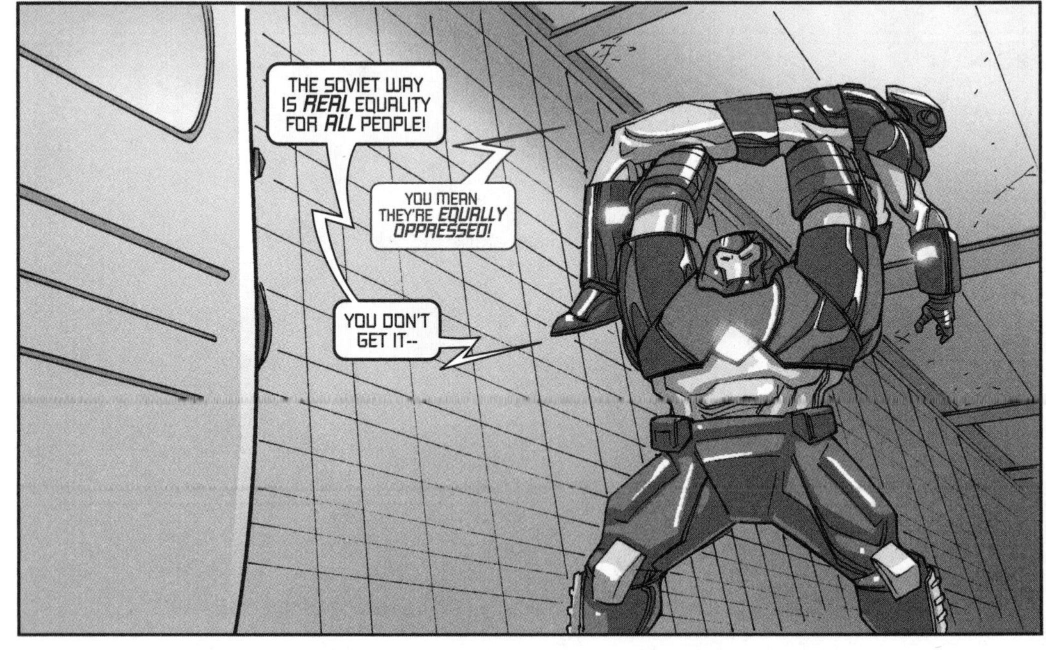
THE SOVIET WAY IS REAL EQUALITY FOR ALL PEOPLE!
YOU MEAN THEY'RE EQUALLY OPPRESSED!
YOU DON'T GET IT--

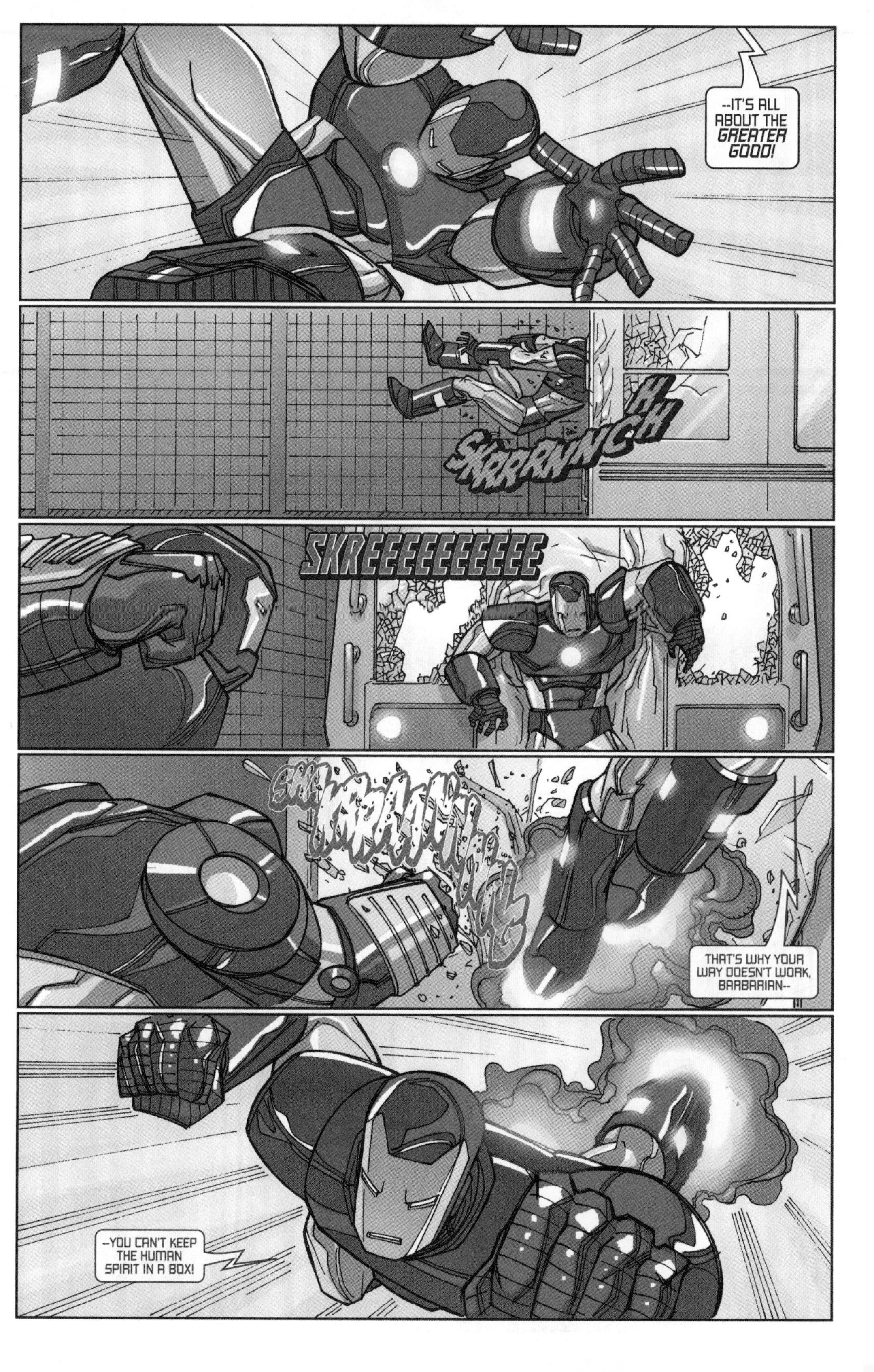
--IT'S ALL ABOUT THE *GREATER GOOD!*
SKREEEEEEEEEEE
THAT'S WHY YOUR WAY DOESN'T WORK, BARBARIAN--
--YOU CAN'T KEEP THE HUMAN SPIRIT IN A BOX!

CAN'T JUST PLAY DEFENSE AND WAIT FOR HIM TO MAKE A MISTAKE ANYMORE...
...HAVE TO STAND UP TO HIM AND FORCE ONE.
STRENGTH LEVEL: 98.95%
KLANG!
CONTACT INITIATED.
TANG!
BANG!
GRAAAH!
FROOOOOOM
ALL OF YOU, GET OUT NOW! THERE'S NO TIME TO LOSE!
GO ON. YOUR REPULSOR IS NO MATCH FOR ME NOW!
I KNOW.
MAGNETIC GRAPPLERS ARMED. INTENSITY: 100%

AHHHHHHHHHHHHHHHH!
THAT'LL STOP HIM...
FLAMETHROWER INTENSITY 100%
PULSE BEAM INTENSITY 100%
REPULSOR INTENSITY 100%
...BUT IT'LL TAKE EVERYTHING I HAVE TO KNOCK HIM DOWN!
TASER INTENSITY 100%
LASER INTENSITY 100%

IT'S OVER.
DEET
YOU'RE SO ARROGANT, STARK...
...YOU CAN'T SEE HOW MUCH ALIKE WE ARE. WE BOTH LIVE IN WORLDS OF UNCOMPROMISING BLACK AND WHITE.
YOU CAN'T SEE THAT YOUR ENEMIES FEEL THEIR CAUSE IS JUST AS RIGHTEOUS AS YOU DO YOURS.
YOU CAN'T SEE THAT YOUR VILLAIN IS SOMEONE'S HERO. SOMEONE'S FATHER, BROTHER, SON AND FRIEND. IT'S NOT OVER. IT'S NEVER OVER...
DEET DEET
...BECAUSE FOR EVERY ONE OF US THAT DIES, THERE ARE MORE WHO WILL SEEK VENGEANCE.
AND THAT'S WHY, UNLIKE YOU...
DEET DEET DEET
...I'M WILLING TO DIE FOR MY BELIEFS.
NO!
DEET DEET DEET
DEET
HE ACTIVATED THE SELF-DESTRUCT!
HA HA HA HA HA HA HA HA!!
DEET DEET

W 47 ST
THRAKKA BOOM!
A FORCE FIELD.
NOW YOU'VE SAVED MY LIFE TWICE.
I WON'T STOP YOU FROM MAKING IT UP TO ME.
TONY!
THERE'S NO MISTAKING THIS TIME...
THAT'S STARK? IN THE ARMOR?
YOU OKAY, MAN?
I CAN'T LIE, I'VE HAD BETTER DAYS.
...THIS IS JIM RHODES.
MY BEST FRIEND.
"I CALLED THIS PRESS CONFERENCE TO DO SOMETHING I'VE NEVER DONE BEFORE (AND HOPE TO NEVER DO AGAIN)--"

APOLOGIZE.
FOR THE PAST FEW MONTHS I LET MY EGO GET IN THE WAY OF GOOD JUDGMENT. IT COST ME MY COMPANY AND ALMOST MY *LIFE.*
I WAS SO WRAPPED UP IN MYSELF THAT I FORGOT THE PRINCIPLE THAT I'VE BUILT MY ENTIRE CAREER ON--
WEAPONS DON'T KILL PEOPLE, *PEOPLE* KILL PEOPLE.
I WAS SO ARROGANT I THOUGHT THAT IF I STOPPED MAKING WEAPONS I COULD SOLVE THE WORLD'S PROBLEMS. BUT THE WORLD'S NOT THAT BLACK AND WHITE.
THE REALITY IS THAT *ANYTHING* IN THE WRONG HANDS CAN BE USED FOR EVIL...
...EVEN THE PEACEKEEPER ARMOR.
SO, EFFECTIVE IMMEDIATELY, I'M RE-OPENING *STARK ENTERPRISES* AND MOVING BACK TO NEW YORK. I'M GOING TO DEDICATE MYSELF TO BUILDING SAFER WEAPONS...
...WITH BETTER TARGETING CAPABILITIES TO CUT DOWN ON COLLATERAL DAMAGE. *THIS* WILL BE MY LEGACY.
THE PEACEKEEPER INITIATIVE WILL CONTINUE, HOWEVER. WHILE I'M OUT EAST, MY BUSINESS ASSOCIATE--
--MY *FRIEND*--
--JIM RHODES WILL OVERSEE THE PROJECT AS PRESIDENT OF *STARK ENTERPRISES...*
...AND HE'LL ANSWER ALL YOUR QUESTIONS RIGHT NOW.
I HAVE A PLANE TO CATCH.
TONY!
TONY!
TONY! OVER HERE!
TONY!
TONY!
TONY!
TONY! OVER HERE!
TONY! OVER HERE! TONY, JUST ONE QUESTION!
WHAT DO YOU HAVE TO SAY ABOUT CONGRESSMAN WYNDHAM'S SUDDEN RESIGNATION?

"NO COMMENT."
YOUR JET'S WAITING ON THE RUNWAY, AND I SCHEDULED A RADIO INTERVIEW WITH MATT AND BRIAN. OH--AND YOUR CALL IS WAITING IN THE CAR.
WHAT AM I GOING TO DO WITHOUT YOU, PEPPER?
OH, PLEASE. AFTER YOU INTERVIEW ALL OF THOSE WOMEN FOR MY JOB, YOU WON'T EVEN REMEMBER MY NAME.
BESIDES, RHODEY NEEDS ME MORE THAN YOU DO RIGHT NOW-- AT LEAST UNTIL HE SETTLES IN.
I KNOW THIS BUSINESS BETTER THAN ANYONE-- INCLUDING YOU.
OH, BELIEVE ME...
...I KNOW.
STARK!
SORRY TO KEEP YOU WAITING, VICTOR...
...BUT I WANT TO THANK YOU FOR YOUR HELP. I HAVE TO ADMIT, IT WAS CLEVER OF YOU TO HAVE ME DO YOUR DIRTY WORK.
YOU ARE NOT AS DUMB AS YOU LOOK, STARK. YES, IT'S TRUE, I KNEW ABOUT THE BARBARIAN'S PLAN ALL ALONG.
SO WHY DID YOU HELP ME?
BECAUSE IF ANYONE WILL BRING YOU TO YOUR KNEES, IT WON'T BE SOME STALE, COLD WAR LEFTOVERS...
...IT WILL BE ME.
BRING IT ON, DOOM. BRING IT ON.
THE END

MARVEL
© 1987 MARVEL COMICS GROUP
$1.25 US
$1.75 CAN
225
DEC
02454
APPROVED BY THE COMICS CODE AUTHORITY

IRON MAN

THEY STOLE HIS TECHNOLOGY...
... AND NOW IT'S
TOTAL WAR!
BRIGHT-LAYTON

Stan Lee PRESENTS: THE INVINCIBLE IRON MAN®
THIS IS HOW IT BEGINS: IN THE OPEN SKY OVER SOUTHERN CALIFORNIA, A MAN IN MICROCIRCUITED ARMOR RACES AGAINST DEATH. IN DAYS, OR PERHAPS WEEKS, IT WILL ALL BE OVER.
BUT THE MAN INSIDE THE RED-AND-SILVER BATTLESUIT WILL NEVER BE THE SAME.
MISSILES ARE OF THE STINGER CLASS! SPEED: 300 MILES PER HOUR! CARRYING WARHEADS THAT COULD BLOW AN F-16 IN HALF!
NO PROBLEM...
STARK WARS!

I'LL JUST USE A MENTAL COMMAND--
--TO CYBERNETICALLY TRIGGER MY BOOT THRUSTERS--
--AND LET THE MISSILES COLLIDE WHERE I WAS A SECOND AGO!

AH-HA! TWO MORE! AND LOOKING FOR A TARGET!
WITH A LITTLE HELP FROM THE MAGNETIC TRACTOR BEAMS FROM MY GAUNTLETS, MAYBE I CAN HELP THEM FIND ONE!
NAMELY--

--EACH OTHER!
THAT'S FOUR! AND ACCORDING TO THE READOUTS IN MY HELMET, MY TRACKING SENSORS HAVE LOCATED THE LAST ONE! COMING IN FAST, AT AN ANGLE THAT SHOULD PUT IT RIGHT--

--ABOOOOUUUT...

...THERE!
PWUBOOOOM

FIVE FOR FIVE!
MISSION ACCOMPLISHED!

HOW WAS THAT PRACTICE RUN, GENERAL?
SPECTACULAR, IRON MAN! COMBINED WITH THE "TANK PULL" STUNT YOU'VE WORKED OUT--

--YOUR DEMONSTRATION SHOULD MAKE OUR ARMY BASE OPEN HOUSE THE CHARITY EVENT OF THE YEAR! YOU HAVE OUR SINCERE APPRECIATION.
IT'S MY-- AND STARK ENTERPRISES'-- PLEASURE. NOW, IF YOU'LL EXCUSE ME...?

TOO BAD TONY COULDN'T BE HERE.
I'M SURE MR. STARK WOULD HAVE LIKED TO, MS. SINCLAIR--

"--BUT HE HAD TO OVERSEE A NEW ATTACK WARNING SYSTEM HIS COMPANY IS DEVELOPING FOR US. AND TO DO THAT--
"--HE NEEDED TO MAN AN ISOLATED MOBILE MONITORING STATION AT THE EDGE OF THE BASE!"

EVERYTHING A-OK, RHODEY?
JUST GREAT, TONY!

WHEN THE PENTAGON GETS THE RESULTS OF THIS NEW WARNING GEAR, IT'LL KNOCK THEIR OLIVE DRAB SOCKS OFF!
GOOD. DEFENSE CONTRACTS ARE TOUGH TO COME BY WHEN YOU REFUSE TO MANUFACTURE MUNITIONS.
BUT THEY'RE ESSENTIAL TO THE GROWTH OF A YOUNG COMPANY LIKE STARK ENTERPRISES!

I JUST HOPE THE WASHINGTON BIGWIGS DON'T FIND OUT THAT THESE TESTS WERE RUN BY TONY STARK'S *PILOT*!
YOU'VE BEEN MORE THAN A "PILOT" FOR SOME TIME, RHODEY. BESIDES--
--IT WOULD BE SORT OF HARD FOR *ME* TO RUN THE TESTS SINCE I *WAS* THE TESTS!

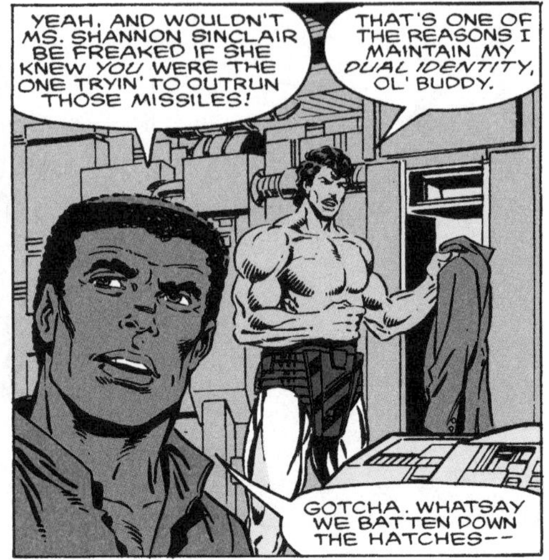
YEAH, AND WOULDN'T MS. SHANNON SINCLAIR BE FREAKED IF SHE KNEW *YOU* WERE THE ONE TRYIN' TO OUTRUN THOSE MISSILES!
THAT'S ONE OF THE REASONS I MAINTAIN MY *DUAL IDENTITY*, OL' BUDDY.
GOTCHA. WHATSAY WE BATTEN DOWN THE HATCHES--

"--AND GET THIS SHOW ON THE ROAD!"
WERE THE TEST RESULTS *SATISFACTORY*, MR. STARK?

BEYOND EXPECTATIONS, SIR. I THINK I CAN SAFELY SAY THAT YOUR SUPERIORS WILL BE *DELIGHTED*!
EXCELLENT!

YOU'RE A SWEETHEART FOR BEING SO PATIENT, SHANNON. NOW HOW ABOUT THAT *LUNCH* I PROMISED. LIKE SEAFOOD?
LOVE IT.
GOOD. I HAPPEN TO OWN A LITTLE PLACE WHERE THEY HAVE THE BEST *ALASKAN KING CRAB* IN THE WORLD. I'LL HAVE RHODEY FLY US THERE.

SOUNDS WONDERFUL. WHAT'S THIS LITTLE PLACE CALLED?
NOME.

APPARENTLY, THE MEAL IS A GOOD ONE. IT IS TWO DAYS BEFORE TONY STARK RETURNS TO STARK ENTERPRISES HEADQUARTERS NORTH OF LOS ANGELES.
AND THERE, IN THE SUB-BASEMENT LABS BENEATH THE ADMINISTRATION BUILDING, AS THE SUN RISES ON ANOTHER FLAWLESS CALIFORNIA DAY...
FASCINATING. I WANTED TO EXAMINE THE ARMOR CLAY WILSON WORE AS FORCE EVER SINCE I CONFISCATED IT FROM HIM, SINCE HE GAVE UP TERRORISM AND WENT STRAIGHT.*
BUT I HAVEN'T HAD TIME UNTIL NOW. THIS CIRCUITRY IS AMAZINGLY SOPHISTICATED! I'VE ALWAYS WONDERED WHERE CRIMINALS GOT SUCH ADVANCED TECHNOLOGY, BUT THIS IS--
*SEE IRON MAN #223-224.

--HUH. THAT WEAPONS ACTIVATION GRID LOOKS LIKE... NO.
IT COULDN'T POSSIBLY--

--OH, MY LORD! IT...
...IT IS!

ONE HOUR LATER, AS JIM RHODES TAKES A PRIVATE ELEVATOR TO THE HIGHLY SECURED SUB-BASEMENT COMPLEX
WHAT THE--?! THAT NOISE COMIN' FROM THE LAB! SOUNDS LIKE SOMEONE'S TEARIN' THE PLACE APART!

SOMEONE IS!
IT'S HERE SOMEWHERE! I KNOW IT IS!
I'VE GOT TO FIND IT!

HE'S EITHER GONE CRAZY, OR GONE BACK TO THE BOTTLE! EITHER WAY--
--IT'S BAD NEWS!
UH, CHIEF? YOU WANNA GIVE ME THAT CROWBAR?

NO! I'VE GOT TO FIND IT!
GOT TO DESTROY IT!

I THINK MAYBE YOU'VE DESTROYED *ENOUGH* FOR ONE DAY! COME ON, NOW, EASE UP!
EASE UP?!
EASE UP?!

YEAH.
EASE UP.
SORRY, JIM. I'M A LITTLE UPSET.
I NOTICED.

IT'S GONE NOW, ANYWAY. I GUESS, INSIDE, I KNOW THAT.
I'VE RUN EVERY SCAN, LOOKED EVERYWHERE I COULD THINK OF.
IT'S JUST NOT *HERE* ANY MORE.
WHAT "IT", CHIEF?

A *BUG*. I WAS CHECKING FORCE'S ARMOR. SOME OF THE DEVICES, SOME OF THE *MOST ESSENTIAL* TECHNOLOGY--

--IS *MINE!*
WHAT?

CERTAIN CIRCUITS ARE BASED ON MY TOP SECURITY *IRON MAN* SYSTEMS, SECRETS I GUARDED SO CLOSELY THAT I DIDN'T EVEN CHANCE *PATENTING* THEM!
SOMEHOW, SOMEONE MUST HAVE BUGGED MY LAB, *STOLEN* THE TECHNOLOGY, AND APPLIED IT TO *FORCE!*
WHICH MEANS THAT ALL THE *DAMAGE* HE CAUSED, EVERY BIT OF PAIN, OF SUFFERING...

...FALLS SQUARELY ON MY SHOULDERS!

AND WORSE, THAT COULD JUST BE THE TIP OF THE ICEBERG! WHAT IF FORCE WASN'T THE ONLY ONE USING THAT STOLEN TECHNOLOGY?
WHAT IF TWO PEOPLE USED IT? A DOZEN? A HUNDRED!
HOLD ON, CHIEF--

--DON'T BE SO HARD ON YOURSELF. IT WASN'T YOUR FAULT.
THE ONLY WAY THAT TECHNOLOGY COULD HAVE BEEN TAKEN WAS IF I WAS CARELESS, JIM.

AND THAT'S NOBODY'S FAULT BUT MY OWN.

I'VE TAPPED INTO THE WEST COAST AVENGERS DATA-BANK, CALLED UP A LIST OF ARMORED CRIMINALS, ANYONE WHO COULD POSSIBLY HAVE BENEFITED FROM AN INFUSION OF MY--AH! IT'S PRINTING NOW!
TITANIUM MAN...

"THE BEETLE...
"...SHOCKWAVE..."
"...DOCTOR DOOM...
"...STILT-MAN...
"...THE CRIMSON DYNAMO...
"...THE CONTROLLER...
"...THE MAULER...
"...THE RAIDERS...
"...PROFESSOR POWER...
"...TITANIUM MAN.
"THE LIST GOES ON.
"AND ON..."

HOW MANY? HOW MANY HAVE DRAWN BLOOD WITH *MY* SWORD?
MAYBE *NONE* OF 'EM, CHIEF! BEFORE WE GO JUMPIN' THE GUN, SHOULDN'T WE GET THE REAL SCOOP FROM THE *HORSE'S MOUTH*?
I'LL DRIVE. OKAY...?

AND SOON, IN AN EMPLOYEE PARKING LOT NEARBY...
MR. STARK? OH, MR. STARK!

I WANTED TO CATCH YOU BEFORE YOU LEFT, TO REMIND YOU OF IRON MAN'S DEMONSTRATION AT THE ARMY BASE THIS AFTER-NOON.
IT'S QUITE A P.R. COUP--
--AND I WOULDN'T WANT YOU TO FORGET.

PUBLIC RELATIONS IS YOUR JOB, MS. PEARSON, AND YOU DO IT QUITE WELL. BUT THE WORLD ISN'T PERFECT.
SOMETHING IMPORTANT HAS COME UP.

I'M AFRAID WE MAY HAVE TO CANCEL IRON MAN'S APPEARANCE.
WHA--?
JIM?
TAKE IT EASY, HON. I KNOW HOW HARD YOU WORKED ON THIS.

I'LL HAVE A TALK WITH THE BOSS, OKAY?
RIGHT.
BRRR! SURE CAN GET CHILLY IN SOUTHERN CALIFORNIA SOMETIMES!
FINE.

NONETHELESS, THE SUN IS SHINING WARMLY A SHORT WHILE LATER OVER BARSTOW ELECTRONICS, A DIVISION OF STARK ENTERPRISES. WHERE...
BARSTOW ELECTRI
MS. SEKIDO? YOU, UH WANTED TO SEE ME?

I HOPE THERE ISN'T ANY PROBLEM WITH MY WORK IN THE *ELECTRO-ANALYSIS LAB*?
NO, *CARL*, YOU'VE DONE FINE. IN FACT, THAT'S EXACTLY WHAT I TOLD--

--MR. STARK.
HUH?!
THANK YOU, NANCY. NOW, IF YOU COULD LEAVE US *ALONE* FOR A MOMENT...?
OF COURSE.

TONY! WH-WHAT'S WRONG? I THOUGHT WHEN I CHANGED MY NAME FROM "*CLAY WILSON*" TO "*CARL WALKER*", THAT WOULD BE THE END OF IT!
SO DID I.
JUSTIN HAMMER STILL HAS A CONTRACT OUT ON YOU. AND IF THIS MEETING COMPROMISES YOUR *SECURITY*--

--I'M SORRY. BUT THERE'S SOMETHING I *HAVE* TO KNOW.
THE TECHNOLOGY THAT WENT INTO YOUR *FORCE* ARMOR-- WHERE DID IT COME FROM?

WELL, I DEVELOPED THE CRUDE *PROTOTYPES* MYSELF--
--BUT THE ADVANCED STUFF, THE REALLY *POWERFUL* DESIGNS, WERE SUPPLIED BY *HAMMER*.

I HAVE NO IDEA WHERE *HE* GOT THEM, BUT--
THANK YOU, CLAY. THAT'S ALL.
BUT IT ISN'T. AND HE KNOWS IT.

AND SHORTLY, AS AN IMMACULATE '57 RAG-TOP HEADS FOR THE HIGHWAY...
ONE BRIGHT POINT, AT LEAST: THE TECHNOLOGY IN FORCE'S ARMOR STOPS SHORT OF WHAT I'VE GOT IN MY RED-AND-SILVER IRON MAN SUIT.
THAT MEANS THE BUGS WERE PROBABLY PLANTED IN MY OLD STARK INTERNATIONAL LABS BACK ON LONG ISLAND.

BUT I STILL DON'T KNOW HOW HAMMER COULD HAVE GOTTEN AWAY WITH PLANTING THEM.
AND UNTIL I DO, I CAN'T BE SURE THAT HE WON'T DO IT AGAIN!

MAYBE YOU SHOULD DO SOMETHING BESIDES THINK ABOUT IT, CHIEF. SOMETHING TO CLEAR YOUR MIND.
LIKE MAYBE THAT CHARITY GIG AT THE BASE.
YEAH. I GUESS.

BUT THOUGH TONY STARK'S RESPONSE MAY SEEM LESS THAN ENTHUSIASTIC, HE RECOGNIZES THE WISDOM IN HIS FRIEND'S WORDS. AND SO, THAT AFTERNOON AT KIRKLAND ARMY BASE...
THAT'S RIGHT, FOLKS. YOU'RE THE FIRST CIVILIANS IN THE WORLD TO SEE THE NEW SP-4 TURBO-TANK! BETTER KNOWN BY ITS NICKNAME--

--THE DEVASTATOR!

THE SP-4 IS ONE OF THE *STRONGEST* WEAPONS IN OUR COUNTRY'S ARSENAL! THAT CART IT'S PULLING IS LOADED WITH *TONS* OF SCRAP METAL! AND YET THE DEVASTATOR POSES NO *HAZARD* TO ITS DRIVER--
--BECAUSE THERE *IS* NONE!

THE REMOTE-CONTROLLED VEHICLE IS PILOTED BY AN OPERATOR WHO CAN BE STATIONED *MILES* FROM ANY COMBAT ZONE!

BUT NOW, TO HELP DEMONSTRATE THE DEVASTATOR'S CAPABILITIES, I'D LIKE TO INTRODUCE OUR *SPECIAL GUEST*: THE ONE, THE ONLY, THE INVINCIBLE--

--IRON MAN!
YAAAY!
WOW!
A REAL *AVENGER*!

YOU'VE SEEN HOW STRONG THE SP-4 IS. AND AS SOON AS TECHNICIANS FINISH ATTACHING THOSE *TITANIUM STEEL CHAINS*, WE'LL FIND OUT HOW STRONG OUR OLD FRIEND "SHELL-HEAD" IS!

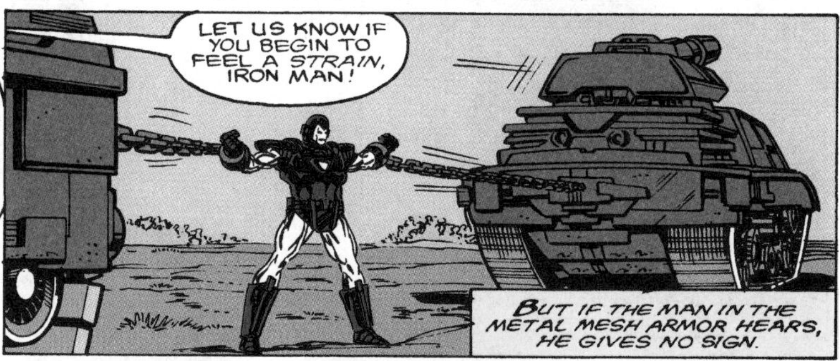
LET US KNOW IF YOU BEGIN TO FEEL A *STRAIN*, IRON MAN!
BUT IF THE MAN IN THE METAL MESH ARMOR HEARS, HE GIVES NO SIGN.

FOR THE STRESS HE FEELS COMES MORE FROM HIS SOUL THAN HIS CORDING MUSCLES.
HIS EYES LOSE FOCUS. IMAGES OF SOLDIERS AND WEAPONS BLUR. AND IT IS ONLY IN HIS MIND THAT HE NOW SEES--

--PICTURES.

PICTURES OF A YOUNG MAN, AN INVENTOR, EAGER TO END AN UNSAVORY WAR WITH INNOVATIVE WEAPONS OF HIS OWN DESIGN.

AN IDEALISTIC MAN WHO INSTEAD FALLS PREY TO THE EXPLOSIVE STRATEGY OF AN UNSEEN ENEMY!

WOUNDED AND CAPTURED, THE YOUNG MAN IS FORCED TO WORK FOR THAT ENEMY. BUT WHILE HIS BODY IS DAMAGED, HIS MIND REMAINS WHOLE--

--AND THROUGH SUBTERFUGE AND GENIUS, HE CREATES HIS OWN AVENUE OF ESCAPE: A BULKY SUIT OF ELECTRIC ARMOR THAT WILL SOON BE KNOWN AS--
--IRON MAN!

AT LONG LAST, THE WAR ENDS. THE YOUNG MAN GROWS BOTH IN YEARS AND IN SPIRIT--
STARK
INTERNATIONAL
--DEDICATING HIMSELF TO THE POSITIVE ASPECTS OF LIFE, THROUGH HIS BRILLIANCE AND BUSINESS ACUMEN--

--AS WELL AS HIS COURAGEOUS SECRET LIFE AS THE HEROIC AVENGER CALLED IRON MAN.

THROUGH TIME, HIS FACADE--THE OUTER MAN--CHANGES. BUT THE PURPOSE AND WILL OF THE HUMAN BEING INSIDE NEVER FALTERS. ALL OF WHICH COMBINE TO MAKE HIS CURRENT SITUATION--

--INTOLERABLE!
SO WHAT GOOD DID IT DO? FOR ALL MY EFFORTS, THE VERY TECHNOLOGY I DEVISED TO HELP PEOPLE HAS BEEN RESPONSIBLE FOR UNTOLD HARM!

AND THERE'S NOT A THING I CAN DO ABOUT IT! NOT A BLOODY... BLASTED...

...THING!
SSHWIP
SSHWIP

KWUMPSH
AW, GEEZ...!

AWESOME, SHELL-HEAD!
WHAT A SHOW!

WHAT THE DEVIL HAPPENED?!
SORRY, GENERAL. IT WAS A, UM, MISCALCU-LATION.
STARK ENTERPRISES WILL PAY FOR DAMAGES.
YOU BET YOUR TIN BUTT THEY WILL, MISTER!

MORNING-- OR PERHAPS MOURNING WOULD BE MORE APROPOS-- COMES TO STARK ENTERPRISES...
NO, SIR--
--I'D SAY "NIGHTMARE" WAS TOO MILD A TERM!

MY PUBLICITY DEPARTMENT IS TREADING A MICRO-THIN LINE, TRYING TO ABSOLVE S.E. OF ANY BLAME IN THAT ARMY BASE INCIDENT--
--WITHOUT IMPLICATING THE MILITARY AT THE SAME TIME!
MR. STARK
DO YOUR BEST, MARCY. I'LL TALK TO IRON MAN, SEE THAT IT DOESN'T HAPPEN AGAIN.

GOOD. I'LL MAKE SURE YOU GET AN UPDATE BY THIS AFTERNOON.
JUST A SEC, MARCY. I'LL GO WITH YOU.

YOU GONNA BE OKAY, CHIEF? YOU LOOK LIKE A BALLOON WITH A SLOW LEAK!
HMM?

OH.
SURE.
JUST NEED A LITTLE TIME OFF, THAT'S ALL.
I'M FINE.

AND THUS, THAT EVENING AT THE WORLD PREMIERE OF THE CONTROVERSIAL NEW FILM, "DARK ANGEL"...
DARK ANGEL
STEVEN SAYS THIS COULD BE THE NEW "PLATOON", TONY. IT TREATS TERRORISTS WITH INCREDIBLE REALISM!

AND I'M SO GLAD YOU'RE MY DATE! IF YOU HADN'T INTRODUCED ME TO STEVEN,* I WOULDN'T HAVE THAT PART IN HIS NEW FILM!
I'M HAPPY IT WORKED OUT, BRIE.
*IN IRON MAN #222.

MOST PEOPLE SMILE WHEN THEY'RE HAPPY. SOMETHING WRONG?
NOT AT ALL. I'M...
...FINE.

SEATS ARE LOCATED. THE AUDIENCE FALLS HUSH. AND AFTER A SHORT SPEECH BY AN ASSOCIATE PRODUCER, HOUSE LIGHTS DIM--

--AND IMAGES BEGIN TO PASS UPON THE SILVER-SURFACED SCREEN.
IMAGES OF DESTRUCTION, DEVASTATION...SHATTERED LIVES.

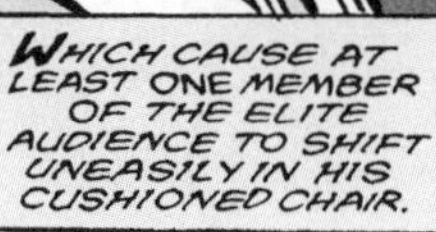
WHICH CAUSE AT LEAST ONE MEMBER OF THE ELITE AUDIENCE TO SHIFT UNEASILY IN HIS CUSHIONED CHAIR.

FOR THE FILM-MAKERS HAD SOUGHT REALISM IN DEPICTING THE EFFECTS OF TERROR ON INNOCENTS.
WEST BELT MALL
AS WELL AS THE CULPABILITY OF THOSE RESPONSIBLE.

AND, IT APPEARS, THEY HAVE SUCCEEDED.

WOW! STRONG STUFF! COULD ALMOST PUT YOU OFF BUTTERED POPCORN FOR LIFE, HUH, TONY?
TO--

--NY?

HEY!
SORRY, BRIE. MUST HAVE BEEN THE, UM, ESCARGOTS AT DINNER.
YOU GO AHEAD AND FINISH THE MOVIE.

NAH. I'VE KIND OF LOST INTEREST. WANT TO GO TO MY PLACE FOR AN ALKA-SELTZER?
OR SOMETHING?

THANKS, BUT I THINK A LONG WALK WOULD BE BETTER FOR ME. I APPRECIATE YOUR UNDERSTANDING. I'LL CALL YOU, OKAY?
WELL, IF YOU'RE SURE I CAN'T HELP?
REALLY...

...I'M FINE.

THE EVENING GROWS OLDER. WHILE AT THE EXCLUSIVE SUNCREST CONDOMINIUM COMPLEX NORTH OF HOLLYWOOD...
I HAD A GOOD TIME, JIM. BUT I WOULD HAVE HAD A BETTER ONE--

--IF *YOU'D* BEEN THERE *WITH* ME!
BUT I *WAS*-- OH. I GET IT. SORRY, MARCY--
--MY MIND'S BEEN WANDERIN' A LOT LATELY.

AN' SPEAKIN' OF "LATE", THAT JERK'S STARTIN' TO GET ON MY *NERVES*, WORKIN' ON HIS HOTSHOT FIREBIRD AT ALL HOURS.
VROOOM

HEY, ACE! PEOPLE *LIVE* HERE! HOW 'BOUT *COOLIN'* IT!
HOW 'BOUT MINDIN' YER OWN *BUSINESS*!

VA ROOOOM

THAT DOES IT! I'M GONNA CRAM THAT *TIMIN' LIGHT* RIGHT WHERE IT BELONGS!
JIM! DON'T! LET'S GO INSIDE, OKAY?

NOW WHAT'S GOING ON? I'VE NEVER *SEEN* YOU SO EDGY!
AH, IT'S THE BOSS. HE'S GOT TROUBLES. *BAD* ONES. AND I DON'T KNOW HOW HE'S GONNA HANDLE 'EM.

I GUESS I'M *WORRIED*.
I AM, TOO. MAYBE WE CAN WORK ON IT TOGETHER. THAT IS...

...*TOMORROW?*
YEAH.
TOMORROW.

BUT TOMORROW COMES SLOWLY, STUBBORNLY, TO A MODERN CASTLE PERCHED ON THE ROCKY PACIFIC COAST. WHERE, AT 3 A.M.--

--THE MASTER OF THE MANSE LIES, SILENT, HIS SATIN SHEETS FEELING UNCHARACTERISTICALLY COARSE. ANOTHER IRRITANT.
AS IF HE NEEDED ONE.

IT'S NO USE.

I HAVE TO KNOW.

AND SOON, AT A MODEST APARTMENT IN AGOURA...
BRRRING
HMPK?
WHUZZAT?

YEAH? WHUZZA-PROLLEM?

HOW MANY DID YOU KILL, CLAY?

HUH?! WH-WHAT THE--
--TONY?
WITH THE ARMOR... THE TECHNOLOGY...

...HOW MANY DID YOU KILL?
LISTEN, TONY, I-I DON'T KNOW WHY YOU'RE ASKING THIS--

--BUT THAT PART OF MY LIFE IS OVER!
I-I'D RATHER NOT TALK ABOUT IT, OKAY?

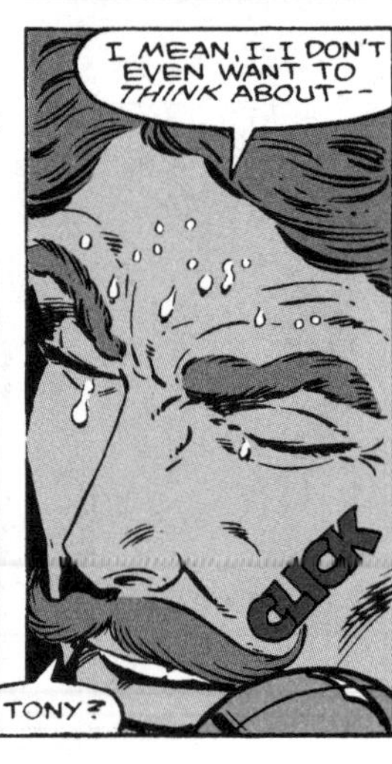
I MEAN, I-I DON'T EVEN WANT TO THINK ABOUT--
CLICK
TONY?

THAT WAS WRONG. I'VE NO RIGHT TO HOUND CLAY. HE'S TRYING TO MAKE UP FOR HIS CRIMES--
--OUR CRIMES...
BUT I CAN'T HELP IT. NO MATTER WHAT I TELL PEOPLE, I'M NOT "FINE".

I'M NOT FINE AT ALL...!

SLEEP REMAINS ELUSIVE, BUT TOMORROW DOESN'T CARE. IT SHOWS UP ANYWAY...
I KNOW YOU'RE SMART, CHIEF--YOU'VE GOT MORE DIPLOMAS THAN MOST FOLKS HAVE SOCKS!
SO WHY'RE YOU DOIN' SOMETHIN' DUMB LIKE THIS?

I MEAN, INFORMATION AIN'T SOLID, BUT STEALIN' IS STEALIN'!
CAN'T BE HELPED, RHODEY. I'VE GOT TO KNOW HOW MUCH HAMMER KNOWS ABOUT IRON MAN. AND ME.

THAT WHY YOU DIDN'T GO TO THE COPS? 'FRAID HAMMER MIGHT TIP THAT YOU'RE IRON MAN?
THAT--

--AND THE FACT THAT I DON'T WANT TO TIP HIM TO WHAT I'M DOING.
OR WHAT I'M AFTER MIGHT CONVENIENTLY DISAPPEAR!

AND AT THIS JUNCTURE, I CAN'T--I WON'T--LET THAT HAPPEN!

AND SOON, AT ACCUTECH RESEARCH AND DEVELOPMENT, ANOTHER OF THE SMALL COMPANIES THAT FORM THE EVER-EXPANDING WEB OF STARK ENTERPRISES...
I HAVE A FAVOR TO ASK, MR. ZIMMER. BUT IT MIGHT NOT BE ENTIRELY... LEGAL.
ACCUTECH

YOU HELPED SAVE MY JOB, MR. STARK-- AND MY DIGNITY.*
TELL ME WHAT YOU WANT ME TO DO.
THANKS, ABE. THIS DISK FILE CONTAINS THE DATA I'VE BEEN ABLE TO GATHER ON JUSTIN HAMMER.
*IN IRON MAN #219.

IT'S IMPOSSIBLE TO NAIL DOWN HAMMER'S EXACT WHEREABOUTS, BUT I HAVE FOUND THAT A COMPANY CALLED "TRANSCORP" IS A FRONT FOR HIS WEST COAST COMMUNICATIONS CENTER. I NEED TO BREAK INTO THEIR DATABASE AND REMOVE A FILE.
YOU'RE THE COMPUTER WHIZ, ABE--CAN WE DO IT?
ACCORDING TO THESE SCHEMATICS, IT WOULD BE EXTREMELY DIFFICULT.

BUT NOT IMPOSSIBLE. I'LL NEED HELP, SOMEONE TO OPEN A "BACK DOOR" WHILE I RETRIEVE THE PROPER FILE.
HE'D HAVE TO BE GOOD--VERY GOOD. AND COMPLETELY TRUSTWORTHY.

HMMM. GOOD WITH ELECTRONICS... AND SOMEONE I CAN TRUST.
THAT'S A NARROW FIELD, BUT MAYBE... JUST MAYBE...

STARK ENTERPRISES...
DROP EVERYTHING ELSE, MRS. ARBOGAST! THIS IS AN EMERGENCY!

I HAVE TO LOCATE AN EX-EMPLOYEE FROM THE OLD DAYS ON LONG ISLAND. A TOP-NOTCH ELECTRONICS TECHNO NAMED SCOTT LANG!
LET'S SEE, HOW CAN WE GO ABOUT IT?

WE COULD START WITH A COMPUTER SWEEP OF PHONE DIRECTORIES IN MAJOR CITIES, EAST TO WEST! YEAH...
...THEN SEND TELEXES TO ALL CORPORATIONS THAT MIGHT EMPLOY SOMEONE LIKE LANG! WHAT ELSE... WHAT--

--AH! AS A LAST DITCH, WE COULD ADVERTISE ON TV! BUY UP LATE-NIGHT SPOTS!

SCOTT WAS ALWAYS WATCHING OLD MOVIES ON--
EXCUSE ME, SIR, THERE IS ONE OTHER ALTERNATIVE.

PERHAPS WE COULD CALL THE PHONE NUMBER ON THIS LETTERHEAD?
WHA--?

WELL, I'LL BE! HE'S FORMED HIS OWN COMPANY!
ELECTRULANG INC.-NO JOB TOO SMALL
Scott Lang
PRESIDENT
CAME IN THE MAIL TODAY SOLICITING BUSINESS.

MRS. ARBOGAST, YOU'RE ONE IN A ZILLION!
WELL, MAYBE ONE IN A MILLION--
--BUT WHO AM I TO ARGUE WITH THE BOSS?

AND SO, AN HOUR LATER AT A PLEASANT HOME IN SUBURBAN LOS ANGELES...
NOK
NOK

WHO IS I--
-GASP-

UNCA TONY! YAAAAY!
-HEH HEH- HI, CASSIE. YOUR POP AROUND?

WHO IS IT, CASS-- TONY?! I-I MEAN, MR. STARK!
"TONY" IS FINE.

SCOTT LANG, THIS IS ABE ZIMMER. YOU ALREADY KNOW RHODEY.
SURE! IT'S GREAT TO SEE YOU AGAIN!

HEY, UNCA TONY, I JUST MADE SOME BURRITO PUDDING FOR MY HOME SCIENCE CLASS! YOU GUYS WANT SOME?

ER, I'M ON A DIET.
I-I'M DRIVIN'!
I JUST -ULP- ATE!
UH, WHY DON'T YOU GO TEST YOUR NEW SKATE-BOARD, SWEET-HEART?
WELL, OKAY! SEE YA LATER!

I GOT THIS ADDRESS FROM YOUR FLYER, SCOTT. THE NEW BUSINESS SOUNDS IMPRESSIVE.
ACTUALLY, YOU'RE LOOKING AT THE NEW BUSINESS!

THINGS GOT KINDA TIGHT BACK EAST, SO CASSIE AND I CAME OUT HERE TO MAKE A NEW START. BUT MOVING'S EXPENSIVE.
I USED THE LAST OF OUR "MAD" MONEY TO HAVE THOSE FLYERS PRINTED UP. I'D HOPED TO GENERATE ENOUGH BUSINESS--
--TO BE ABLE TO RENT A SMALL SHOP.

THEN I MIGHT BE ABLE TO HELP--I CAME HERE TO HIRE YOU.
GREAT!

I HAVE A LITTLE JOB THAT'S RIGHT UP YOUR ALLEY. IT'S KIND OF BORDERLINE AS FAR AS THE LAW IS CONCERNED, BUT--

HOLD ON A SECOND! I'M AN EX-CON, REMEMBER? I SPENT FIVE YEARS OF MY DAUGHTER'S LIFE IN PRISON!
I CAN'T LET THAT HAPPEN AGAIN!

I WOULDN'T ASK IF IT WASN'T IMPORTANT, SCOTT. IF THERE WEREN'T LIVES ON THE LINE.
WE'LL TAKE EVERY PRECAUTION, I PROMISE. AND IF WE'RE SUCCESSFUL, YOU CAN FORGET ABOUT RENTING THAT SHOP.
I'LL BUY YOU ANY STORE YOU WANT!

YOU ALWAYS DID KNOW WHICH STRINGS TO PULL, TONY.
I'M NOT SURE WHETHER TO ADMIRE THAT, OR RESENT IT--BUT WHAT THE HECK.
I'M IN!

YOU CERTAIN THAT WAS A GOOD THING, CHIEF?
IT WAS SCOTT'S DECISION, EVEN IF I DID HELP IT ALONG. AND IF WE GET CAUGHT, I'LL HAVE MY ENTIRE LEGAL DEPARTMENT AT HIS DISPOSAL.
BUT IF YOU'RE ASKING HOW I FEEL ABOUT IT--

--TRY "ROTTEN".

MIDNIGHT: TENSION CRACKLES AROUND STARK ENTERPRISES LIKE UNSEEN FIRE.

WHILE AT A SPECIAL CONSOLE INSIDE...
I CAN UNDERSTAND WHY MR. STARK WANTS TO BE CLOSE TO THE ACTION, TO BETTER SUPERVISE IRON MAN--
--BUT WHY WOULD MR. LANG INSIST ON A MOBILE HOOK-UP ONLY A BLOCK FROM THE OBJECTIVE?
BEATS ME.

MAN SAID IT WAS A TRADE SECRET.
WHOOP-- GETTIN' CLOSE TO SHOWTIME! BETTER CHECK IN!

RHODES HERE. YOU IN POSITION, IRON MAN?
AFFIRMATIVE. TARGET IN SIGHT!

'COURSE, THE TRANSCORP TOWER IS KIND OF HARD TO MISS, EVEN AT THIS ANGLE!

I SHOULD HAVE NO PROBLEM CAUSING THE DISTRACTION MR. ZIMMER REQUIRES AT 12:10 SHARP!

SCOTT? THIS IS RHODEY. ALL SET?
FER SHURE!

SORRY. GUESS CALIFORNIA'S GROWIN' ON ME. BUT DON'T WORRY, I'LL BE INSIDE THE TRANSCORP COMPUTERS ON TIME!
CHECK!

ACTUALLY, THANKS TO MY SHRINK GAS, I REALLY WILL BE "INSIDE" THE COMPUTERS!
I WONDER WHAT TONY WOULD THINK IF HE KNEW HE HAD THE ASTONISHING ANT-MAN ON HIS PAYROLL!

C'MON, WHITMORE! LET'S RIDE!
ER, FLY!
TARK
ERPRISES

BREAKING INTO THE DATABASE THIS WAY IS PROBABLY A BIT MORE CERTAIN. BUT THERE'S ABSOLUTELY NO QUESTION--
--THAT IT'S A LOT MORE FUN!
TRANSCORP.

ACCORDING TO THE SCHEMATICS, THE CHIP ABE WANTS ME TO FIDDLE WITH SHOULD BE--
PREEP
--EH? I'VE TRIPPED SOME SORT OF SENSOR!

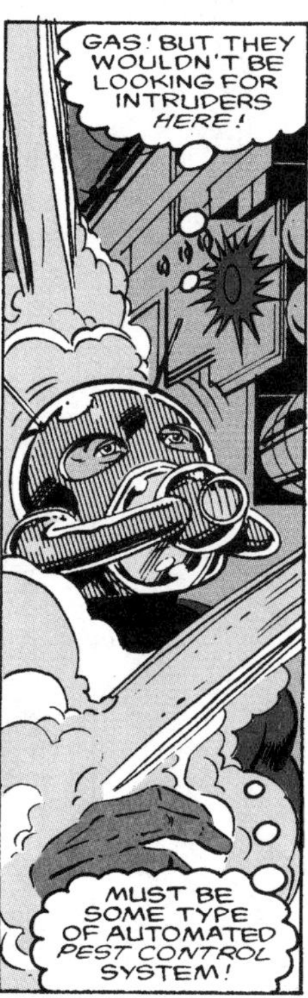
GAS! BUT THEY WOULDN'T BE LOOKING FOR INTRUDERS HERE!
MUST BE SOME TYPE OF AUTOMATED PEST CONTROL SYSTEM!

HOW HUMILIATING!
ZATCH

THERE IT IS! FLIPPING THAT CIRCUIT SHOULD REVERSE THE DATA FLOW--
--FROM INCOMING TO OUTGOING!

ALL SET! NOW I JUST HAVE TO WAIT FOR 12:10--
--AND THAT DISTRACTION!

AN EVENT THAT COMES PRECISELY ON TIME--
--AS AN IRRESISTIBLE FORCE--

--MEETS A NEARLY IMMOVABLE OBJECT!
WHOMP!

WHAT THE--?
EARTHQUAKE!

DONE!

IT'S WORKING!
DATA TRANSFER COMMENCING!

NOW ALL WE NEED IS ENOUGH--
TAK TAKA TAK

"--TIME!"
SHAKING'S STOPPED! MAYBE-- HEY!
WARNING LIGHT!

PROBABLY JUST A SHORT FROM THE TREMOR, BUT WHY TAKE CHANCES?
WE'D BETTER SHUT HER--

"--DOWN!"
PLIP

LATER, IN A PENTHOUSE ATOP THE ADMINISTRATION BUILDING AT STARK ENTERPRISES...
DID WE DO IT? DID WE?
THOSE TRANSCORP FELLAS CAUGHT ON REAL FAST, MR. STARK--
--BUT I THINK WE GOT MOST OF IT.

IT'S ON THIS DISK. I DIDN'T READ IT, JUST LIKE YOU ASKED.
THANKS, ABE.

MY PLEASURE. BY THE WAY, YOU SHOULD GIVE THAT LANG YOUNGSTER A BONUS!
HE WAS TERRIFIC!

A FLOPPY DISK IS INSERTED INTO THE DRIVE UNIT OF A DESKTOP P.C. ACCESS CODES ARE PUNCHED IN. AND--
WELL, I'LL BE--! IT WASN'T HAMMER WHO STOLE THE TECHNOLOGY AFTER ALL! IT WAS--

--SPYMASTER!
SPYMASTER
UH-HUH. AND HE SOLD IT TO HAMMER! HMM, NO MENTION OF MY DUAL IDENTITY. MUST'VE BEEN HIS ACE-IN-THE-HOLE BEFORE IT DIED WITH HIM!*
*IN ISSUE #220.

THAT THE LIST O' FOLKS HAMMER DOLED THE STUFF OUT TO?
BEETLE
CONTRO
PROFESS
RAIDERS
YEAH. DANGEROUS MEN. EVERY ONE OF WHOM HAS CAUSED MORE SORROW AND PAIN THAN YOU CAN IMAGINE.

WITH MY INVENTIONS!
WHAT'RE YA GONNA DO, CHIEF?
THAT'S EASY, JIM: WHATEVER I HAVE TO.

THUS, THE NEXT DAY AS TONY STARK SUMMONS REPRESENTATIVES FROM HIS LEGAL AND CLERICAL STAFFS...
THE TECHNOLOGY IN QUESTION IS MINE-- AND I WANT IT BACK! I WANT YOU TO DO EVERYTHING IN YOUR POWER, USE EVERY LEGAL TRICK!
AND TRY TO BE DISCREET. THIS KIND OF PUBLICITY WE DON'T NEED!

BERT, YOU'RE TO HANDLE THE INTERNATIONAL ASPECTS PERSONALLY. NOTHING-- I REPEAT: NOTHING--IS TO HAVE A HIGHER PRIORITY!
YES, SIR!

YOU THINK GOING THROUGH THE COURTS WILL DO ANY GOOD?
I DON'T KNOW. BUT I HAVE TO GIVE THE LEGAL SYSTEM A CHANCE.
OF COURSE--

--THAT DOESN'T MEAN THAT IRON MAN HAS TO SIT AROUND ON HIS THUMBS IN THE MEANTIME.

AND INDEED HE DOESN'T--AS SOON BECOMES APPARENT SEVERAL NIGHTS LATER IN DOWNTOWN L.A.
WHERE AN UPPER FLOOR OF A HIGH-RISE OFFICE BUILDING RECEIVES A VISITOR--

--WHO DOES NOT HAVE AN APPOINTMENT!
TONK
TINK

DON'T KNOW WHY I'M BOTHERING TO SCAN FOR ALARMS.
PEEPEEP
WHO'D TAKE PRECAUTIONS AGAINST A BREAK-IN...

--7 STORIES UP!
THAT'S WHAT MAKES STILT-MAN SO SUCCESSFUL!

I'LL HAVE THOSE DOCUMENTS AND BE LONG GONE BEFORE--EH?
TAP TAP

SOMEONE ON THE SIDEWALK? BETTER ZOOM IN AND SEE WHAT--
--AW, NO!

YI-YI-YI!
KA-BLANG

CHONK
WHEW

THAT WAS A SUCKER PUNCH, TIN MAN! BUT IT DIDN'T HURT MY HYDRAULIC LEGS!

AS YOU'LL FIND OUT WHEN THEY SMASH YOU RIGHT THROUGH THE SIDE-WAL--

WHOOOK--!
SPLAM

WHAT AM I, CRAZY? THAT GUY'S WAY OUTTA MY LEAGUE!
BETTER JETTISON MY STILTS AND GET THE HECK OUTTA HERE!

WELL, THAT'S A NEW TWIST.

WH-BONK

NOT A GOOD ONE, MIND YOU, BUT A NEW ONE...!

NOW TO MAKE SURE HE NEVER USES THIS ARMOR TO HARM ANYONE AGAIN!
PLAP

SO LONG, "KAREEM!" I'LL SEE THAT THE POLICE STOP BY TO GIVE YOU A HAND!
SKRAZZLE
POP

THE WEIGHT OF THE WORLD LIES SLIGHTLY LESS HEAVILY ON IRON MAN'S SHOULDERS AS HE ROCKETS UP TO A GENTLY HOVERING HELICOPTER.

WHERE...
HOW'D IT GO?
GREAT! THE DETECTION SCANNER I DEVISED WAS ABLE TO TRACK DOWN THE UNIQUE ELECTRONIC PULSES GIVEN OFF BY MY STOLEN TECHNOLOGY!

SEE THAT FADING BLIP? THAT'S WHAT'S LEFT OF STILT-MAN'S ARMOR!
THEN THE NEGATOR PACK WORKED, TOO, HUH?

LIKE A CHARM. I JUST SLAPPED IT ON AND IT FUSED WIRING AND TURNED PLASTIC TO POWDER! IT'LL RENDER ANY KIND OF MECHANISM EMPLOYING MY CIRCUITRY USELESS!
OF COURSE, NOT ALL OF OUR TARGETS WILL BE SO EASY, BUT WITH A LITTLE LUCK, WE'LL GET THE COURTS TO SKRAG A FEW FOR US!

HOWEVER, THE NEXT MORNING...
SORRY IT'S NOT BETTER NEWS, MR. STARK, BUT OUR MAIN SOURCE OF EVIDENCE IS THAT TRANSCORP COMPUTER FILE--
--AND THE JUDGE HAS DETERMINED THAT IT WAS OBTAINED ILLEGALLY, AND IS THEREFORE INADMISSABLE!

I SEE. WELL, TRY EVERY OTHER ANGLE YOU CAN THINK OF, BERT. KEEP ON IT.
YES, SIR.

AND SO WILL I...!

THUS, TWO DAYS LATER IN DENVER, COLORADO, AT THE SITE OF THE ANNUAL SOLDIER OF FORTUNE CONVENTION...
WINNER OF THE AUTOMATIC WEAPONS COMPETITION FOR THE THIRD YEAR IN A ROW--
SOLDIER OF FORTUNE ANNUAL CONVENTION

--BRENDAN DOYLE! CONGRATULATIONS, BREN!
THE PLEASURE'S ME OWN, LADDIE--ALONG WITH THE TROPHY, O'COURSE.
JUDGE

BANQUET STARTS IN A HALF-HOUR, DOYLE. BETTER CHANGE INTO YOUR FORMAL CAMOS!
RIGHT! BE SEEIN' YE OVER AT THE--

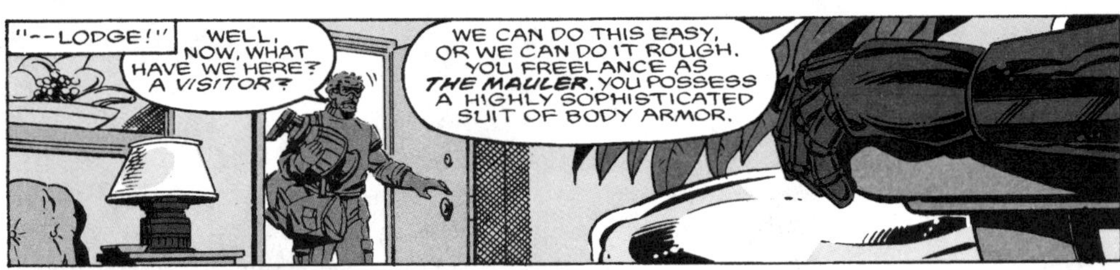
"--LODGE!"
WELL, NOW, WHAT HAVE WE HERE? A VISITOR?
WE CAN DO THIS EASY, OR WE CAN DO IT ROUGH. YOU FREELANCE AS THE MAULER. YOU POSSESS A HIGHLY SOPHISTICATED SUIT OF BODY ARMOR.

I WANT IT.

OH, YE MEAN THIS LITTLE THING? FAITH, LAD, IT'S YOURS!
NO FIGHT?
I GET PAID TA FIGHT, BUCKO.

THAT BATTLESUIT WAS THE SWEETEST MEAL TICKET I EVER HAD! SURE AN' I'M GONNA MISS IT! LEASTWAYS--
--TILL I CAN STEAL MESELF ANOTHER!

CALIFORNIA. THE FOLLOWING WEEK.
I'M SORRY, SIR, BUT DEFENSE ATTORNEYS INSIST THAT THE TECHNOLOGY IN QUESTION WAS NEVER PATENTED! THEY SUGGEST THAT YOUR INVENTIONS ARE IN THE PUBLIC DOMAIN!

THEY'VE EVEN RAISED DOUBT AS TO WHETHER THERE'S BEEN A THEFT AT ALL!
BLAST IT, BERT, I PAY YOU TOP DOLLAR!
AND I EXPECT YOU TO EARN IT! DO SOMETHING!

LITTLE ROUGH ON THE MAN, WEREN'T YOU, CHIEF?
YEAH, I KNOW. I'LL APOLOGIZE LATER. I'M JUST A LITTLE EDGY, KNOWING WHAT WE MIGHT BE ABOUT TO GO UP AGAINST!

INDEED. AND SOON, AT A SUN-WORSHIPER'S MECCA ATTACHED TO AN ABANDONED CHURCH...
THE CONTROLLER HAS BEEN SPOTTED IN SOUTHERN CALIFORNIA, AND THE DETECTION SCANNER INDICATES THAT MY STOLEN TECHNOLOGY IS BEING USED IN THE VICINITY OF THIS TANNING SALON.
WHO'S THIS "CONTROLLER" DUDE?
HE'S AN ARMORED EGOTIST WHO USES CONTROL DISKS TO MAKE INNOCENTS HIS SLAVES! HIS CIRCUITS ARE ATTACHED BIOLOGICALLY, SO I DON'T KNOW IF A NEGATOR PACK WOULD BE SAFE TO USE. WE'LL JUST HAVE TO PLAY IT BY EAR. BUT FIRST--

"--WE'LL NEED TO MAKE SURE WE'RE ON THE RIGHT TRACK!"
MAY I HELP YOU, SIR?
YES, I'M LOOKING FOR SOMETHING IN A SECOND-DEGREE CHARBROIL.

I'LL JUST HELP MYSELF, OKAY?
WAIT! Y-YOU CAN'T GO IN--

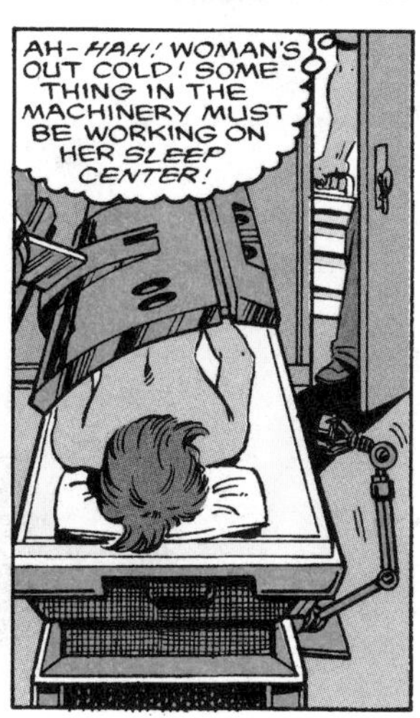
AH-HAH! WOMAN'S OUT COLD! SOME-THING IN THE MACHINERY MUST BE WORKING ON HER SLEEP CENTER!

AND UNLESS I'M VERY WRONG, THAT MECHANICAL ARM HEADING FOR THE BACK OF HER NECK IS ABOUT TO ATTACH--

--A CONTROL DISK! THIS MUST BE THE PLACE!
AND IF WE NEED ANY MORE PROOF--

--I THINK IT JUST SHUFFLED IN FROM THE BACK ROOM!

THOSE MUSCLE-BOYS' EYES LOOK ABOUT AS LIVELY AS A CARP IN THE SAHARA!

THE ONLY WAY TO STOP THOSE ZOMBIES IS TO STOP THE CONTROLLER! BETTER BUY ME SOME TIME, RHODEY!
YOU GOT IT!
K-KLIK

NO! NO GUNS! THESE PEOPLE ARE JUST DUPES!
TRY NOT TO HURT THEM!
"THEM"?! WHAT ABOUT ME?

I CAN THINK OF EASIER WAYS O' GETTIN' A WORKOUT!

I HATE LEAVING RHODEY ON HIS OWN--
--BUT THE ONLY WAY TO END THIS NIGHTMARE IS TO FIND THE CONTROLLER!
AND WITH HIS EGO, I'VE A FEELING THIS "RECRUITING STATION" WASN'T BUILT ADJACENT TO AN OLD TEMPLE BY ACCIDENT! WHICH MEANS THAT THE FIRST PLACE TO LOOK IS--

"--NEXT DOOR!"
WELCOME, IRON MAN! I ASSUMED ONE OF YOU POMPOUS WORLD-SAVERS WOULD LOCATE ME EVENTUALLY!

BUT IT DOESN'T MATTER--MY POWER BASE IS NEARLY COMPLETE!
ONCE ENOUGH OF THESE TREND-FOLLOWING YUPPIES ARE UNDER MY COMMAND, I'LL HAVE THE STRENGTH TO MAKE CALIFORNIA MINE!

EVEN NOW, SEE HOW EASY THEY FOLLOW MY ORDER TO... KILL YOU!
THESE PEOPLE CAN'T HURT ME-- BUT I CAN'T TAKE A CHANCE ON HURTING THEM!

GOT TO BRING THE CONTROLLER INTO THE FIGHT!
THAT WHY YOU'RE INTO POWER, CONTROLLER? BECAUSE YOU'RE NOT MAN ENOUGH TO HANDLE THINGS YOURSELF!

CAN'T SEE IF HE WENT FOR IT!
GOT TO WORK MYSELF OUT FROM UNDER THESE--

YAAAGH!
THAT BOY! CAUGHT BETWEEN US!

H-HIS EYES! THE WAY HIS HEAD LOLLS! HE'S--

--DEAD?

KA-BRASH

SPUTCH

MY WHOLE REASON FOR COMING HERE WAS TO KEEP ANYONE ELSE FROM BEING *HARMED* BY MY TECHNOLOGY!
AND NOW, *BECAUSE* OF THAT TECHNOLOGY, SOMEONE HAS--

--*DIED*!
WHROK

YOU'RE *THROUGH*, CONTROLLER! YOUR REIGN OF TERROR IS GOING TO *END*!

AND I'M--
CHRUNCH

--THE ONE--
THRAK

--TO END IT!
CHUDD

WHA--?
TOO ANGRY! DIDN'T NOTICE THE CONTROLLER'S *WORSHIPERS* CLOSING IN!

CAN'T RISK ANY MORE GETTING IN THE WAY!
SPOING
WHATEVER HAPPENS, CONTROLLER--

--YOU BROUGHT THIS ON *YOURSELF!*

SHHRASSHOW

NEGATOR PACK WORKED! CIRCUITS ARE FUSING! MELTING!
BUT THE CONTROLLER! IS...IS HE...?

OOOUUUUUUHHH.
ALIVE.
BULLY FOR HIM...

THREE DAYS LATER...
MR. HINDEL, SIR.
WHAT IS IT, BERT?
GOOD NEWS, MR. STARK.

MY TEAM HAS MADE A CASE FOR YOUR CIVIL RIGHTS BEING VIOLATED BY THE THEFT OF YOUR UNPATENTED INVENTIONS!
WE CAN'T LINK THE ROBBERIES TO MR. HAMMER--HE'S TOO WELL COVERED--

--BUT WE MAY BE ABLE TO SECURE YOUR RIGHTS TO FUTURE USE OF THE TECHNOLOGY! BEST YET, WE'VE BEEN ABLE TO NAIL DOWN A HEARING DATE:
AUGUST 12, 1989!

WHAT?! DO YOU REALIZE HOW MANY PEOPLE THAT TECHNOLOGY COULD KILL BY THEN?
A-ACTUALLY, SIR, WITH THE CURRENT BACKLOG OF COURT CASES--
--WE WERE QUITE LUCKY TO--

PLEASE LEAVE, MR. HINDEL.
SIR?
GET OUT!

WATCH YOUR STEP, JIM. HE'S IN A BAD ONE TODAY!
THANKS, BERT! I'LL REMEMBER TO DUCK!

WHAT'S UP, CHIEF?
MY PATIENCE. I BELIEVE IN THE LAW, AND IN THE SYSTEM. BUT THE PEOPLE I'M UP AGAINST DON'T.
MAYBE IT'S TIME FOR LIVES TO MEAN MORE THAN RULES.

IT'S A TOUGH DECISION; PERHAPS THE TOUGHEST OF MY LIFE.
BUT WITH THE GOVERNMENT'S SUPPORT, OR ITS HINDRANCE...BY THE LAW, OR AGAINST IT...I'M GOING TO GET BACK WHAT'S MINE.
AND HEAVEN HELP ANYONE WHO GETS IN MY WAY!
NEXT ISSUE: THE QUEST BEGINS! BE HERE!

IRON MAN AND THE ARMOR WARS BLACK AND WHITE ART BY CRAIG ROUSSEAU

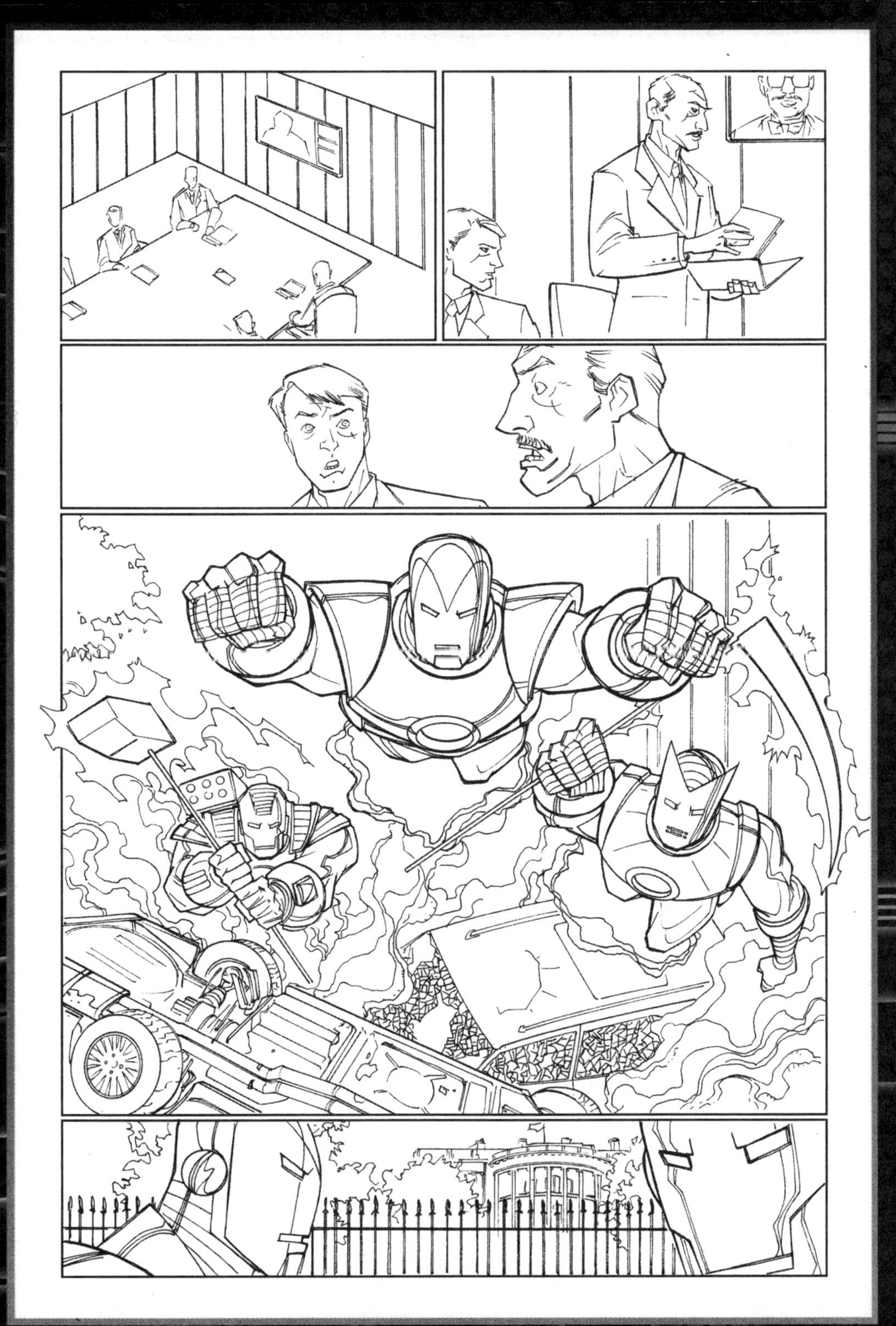